Contents

TELL ME YOUR
BEST STORY

James Patterson
and Emily Raymond

Prologue

*I*F THERE was one thing that could be said about me, one thing almost everyone in my life could agree on, it was this: Anne McWilliams does a lousy job of taking advice.

My mother, when I was eight: *Annie, don't ride your bike down that hill with your shoes untied.*

My dad, when I was sixteen: *Don't waste your hard-earned money on that rust bucket — it won't drive you to the A&P without blowing a gasket.*

My best friend, when I was thirty: *Don't marry Patrick Quinn. Your courtship was way too short, and he's way too hot.*

What I have to say in retrospect (after a broken arm, a broken fuel line, and — you guessed it — a broken heart) is this: A girl should be free to make her own mistakes. That which doesn't kill you, etc., etc.

For thirty-six years I thought I knew what was best, mistakes be damned. But then, all of a sudden, my life turned upside down, and it didn't seem like I knew anything anymore.

Chapter I

A STORM was coming. Even an island transplant like me could tell.

From the deck of my little cottage, thirty yards from the beach, I could see the gray Atlantic churning wildly, furiously, like something alive. The gusting wind whipped my hair into my coffee when I tried to take a sip.

My neighbor Bill was watching the ocean from his deck, too. He turned to me and yelled, "The tropical depression got upgraded to a Category 1 hurricane. Gonna make landfall tonight near Myrtle Beach."

"Kind of exciting!" I called back.

Bill snorted. I could see what he was thinking: *Fool Yankee—she'll probably walk around with that dang camera of hers, trying to take pretty storm pictures.* But I had no intention of doing that. I was going to sit on my couch with a glass of wine and a good book and wait the whole thing out.

"Well, it's probably going to be fine," he allowed, "but it's not going to be fun."

"But Myrtle Beach is over a hundred miles south of us," I pointed out.

Bill glanced up at the sky, then back at me. "You don't know what a hurricane's going to do until it's done it, Anne," he warned. "You'd better cover your windows."

"I'm about to."

"You got supplies? Food, water?"

I nodded. I had bottled water, a well-stocked pantry, and a case of good pinot—I was ready for a *siege*. But I wasn't afraid of the coming weather. I'd lived on this island for two years now with no storms to speak of. Everything was going to be okay.

The first drops of rain began to fall. Like an idiot, I welcomed them.

"Best get moving on them windows," Bill said.

I hurried down below my cottage (like most houses on this North Carolina island, it was built on stilts), and, one by one, hauled up the six big pieces of plywood I needed.

An hour later, I was high on my rickety ladder, struggling with the last unwieldy piece, when the rain started really coming down. Then the wind suddenly got crazy, and it started raining sideways.

Bill came out again and shouted over the gusts. "You need help, Anne?"

"I'm okay—this is the last one," I called.

"I hope Gimme Shellter gets blown out to sea," he yelled.

Gimme Shellter belonged to my other neighbor,

Topher, a software executive from Oklahoma City who'd just planted enormous, spot-lit palm trees all around his brand-new McMansion so it looked like a mini Las Vegas casino. The only good thing to say about Topher was that he was rarely home.

"Worse things could happen," I called back.

The rain stung my face as I wrestled the last window covering into place, banging the wood into tension clips mounted to the window frame. Then I stumbled inside, exhausted and soaking wet.

Maybe I'd been wrong, thinking this was going to be exciting.

Through the tiny glass pane in the front door I could see green sheet lightning flashing over the Atlantic. The clouds had gotten lower, like they were trying to press down against the earth and squash it. The big fronds of Topher's date palms were being ripped off and sent pin-wheeling through the air.

Half an hour later, the water was white with foam and surging up the beach toward my house. Would it crest the small dune, the only thing between me and the open ocean?

The rain was torrential now, and debris flew high into the sky. A trash can someone had forgotten to tie down shot down the beach like a bullet.

It looked as if the wind were trying to tear the world to pieces.

I turned on the TV, but before I'd even found the right station, the power went out.

Like Bill said, things will be fine, they just won't be fun, I reminded myself.

I didn't have a battery-operated radio, so I didn't know that the storm had changed course.

Or that it had gotten bigger and was headed right toward me.

Outside, the wind roared like a freight train. I crawled under the kitchen table, which was shaking right along with the house. How dumb I'd been: I'd thought I'd be drinking a glass of wine on my couch, and here I was, cowering on the rattling floor.

After what felt like forever I got up, my knees weak with fear. Wanting better shelter, I threw every pillow I owned into my bathtub and grabbed my laptop and phone. Something—a tree limb, another trash can, I don't know—crashed into the side of my house. There was another bang as something smaller hit my deck.

I was too scared to look at the ocean again.

I was just about to climb into the bathtub and cover myself with the pillows when the sound of the wind grew quieter.

The rain stopped abruptly.

I stood up again. I crept toward the front door. I paused, and then I opened it.

Looking up at the sky, I could see huge walls of clouds on every side, brilliant white in the sunlight. The air was warm and wet. Only the ocean still surged, just a few feet from the dune.

For a minute, I thought it was over. That I was safe.

But as everyone knows, hurricanes have eyes. And the wind comes back—maybe even stronger.

And pretty soon, it came, flinging needles of sand into my face before I ran back inside.

If I said that hurricane had the same name as the woman my husband left me for—*Claire*—you might not believe me. But it's true.

And if I thought that in losing him, I had lost enough— well, *that* wouldn't turn out to be true at all.

An hour later, I watched Bill's shed fly away like the farmhouse in *The Wizard of Oz*. Through the tiny window in my front door I watched as waves as big as my house crashed ashore only yards away.

My house creaked and shook, trying to stand its ground against the wind. The rain was relentless. Horizontal.

I ran back to my bathroom and shut the door. I crawled into the bathtub and pulled the pillows over me. The wind was screaming banshees. I swear I saw the walls moving, pushing in and out as if they were breathing.

Then something *huge* smashed into my house, and the whole world seemed to shake. The shrieking wind was even louder now. And was that the sound of rain falling right outside the bathroom door? Falling *inside* my house?

The door rattled but held. I burrowed down under

pillows and prayed to anyone who would listen, *Don't let me die. Don't let me die.*

Water—waves or rain—slid under the bathroom door. The wind sounded like a thousand people screaming.

I screamed, too.

Chapter 2

I THOUGHT I'd be swept out to sea in the middle of the night. But I woke on dry land, curled up in my bathtub.

The walls around me still stood, and for a moment I was sure that I'd escaped the storm unscathed. But when I crawled from the tub and stepped into the hall-way, I saw the extent of the destruction. My house wasn't a house anymore — it looked like a pile of debris with a bathroom.

Topher's biggest palm tree, the one that had cost him $15,000, had fallen onto the back half of my cottage and *demolished* it.

I sank down to my knees. I would have thrown up, but there was nothing in my stomach.

It wasn't just losing the house, the sweet little cottage I'd just painted a cheerful yellow. It was my *darkroom,* now crushed under that ridiculous tree. My passion — and my livelihood.

I was probably the only photographer in the south-eastern United States who didn't use a digital camera. I processed the negatives and printed the photos myself—steps that were as much a part of the art as taking the original picture.

Needless to say, I'd uploaded exactly *nothing* to the cloud.

Which meant I had exactly nothing left of my portfolio.

I was too gutted to cry.

"Annie, Annie, are you okay?" Bill called. He stood below the ruined edge of my house with a ladder. "Come down this way," he urged.

Numb, my body vibrating with shock, I climbed down and looked around me. There was a creek running down the street behind my house, and in it bobbed tree branches, a baby stroller, and a laundry basket. At first I thought my car was gone, too, but then I spotted it twenty-five yards north of where I'd parked her, partially submerged in a giant puddle.

Topher's garage roof was gone. Most of Bill's siding had been ripped off, and his deck, like mine, had been swept away.

But it looked like I'd been hit hardest.

"You said everything would be fine," I cried.

Bill's normally stern face seemed to crumple. "I said *probably,*" he reminded me. "Anne, I'm so sorry."

For the first time in over a year, I ached for my ex-husband. I'd ignore Patrick Quinn's wandering eye forever if he'd only come back and help me deal with this mess. And if sometimes, at night, he'd still hold me close.

Bill reached out and roughly patted me on the shoulder. I felt like someone had scooped out my insides, and I had to turn away. I couldn't even bear to look at what else was lost.

And so, wearing ratty sweats and a pair of waders, I headed north toward town.

The beach was covered in trash and the air smelled rank, but the birds were back, pecking around in the wreckage.

The sun came out as I walked, and then, as if by magic, the air filled with butterflies.

My mother would have told me there was a message in this—something about beauty after a storm—but she'd been dead almost twenty years now. And I wouldn't have believed her anyway.

Chapter 3

BARNACLE BILL'S Diner looked like it had been hit hard, too, but then again it had looked that way *before* the hurricane. That was one of the reasons only locals went there. Despite its faded, decrepit exterior, inside it was bright and clean, and almost everyone I knew was tucked into the red vinyl booths, sharing stories about the storm.

When I staggered in, though, the room went quiet. It was clear to everyone that my night had not gone well.

Lorelei and Sam, my best island friends, rushed over. "Are you okay? Was it bad? Tell us what happened," they cried.

I collapsed into a booth.

"Sustenance on its way, stat," Lorelei said. She was a nurse, a marvel of efficiency.

Phil, son of the original Barnacle Bill, brought me three powdered-sugar donuts and a chocolate cruller. I stuffed half of the latter into my mouth at once. If now wasn't a time to stress-eat, I didn't know what was.

"Power's still off, so Mary made coffee on the grill out back," Phil said, handing me a napkin.

I looked up at them gratefully as Mary poured me a cup.

"All you need's a big lobster pot, bottled water, and about two pounds of beans," she explained.

I took a single sip. Then I burst into tears.

Sam slid over to my side of the bench and put her arm around me. "The roof of my store got peeled back," she said. "It looks like the lid of a dang tuna can. What happened to you, baby?"

I waved my hands in the air helplessly. I couldn't speak.

"Phil, make this woman a Bloody Mary," Lorelei called.

"Make that three," Sam added.

"You know I don't have a liquor license, Lo," Phil said.

Lorelei lifted one carefully penciled eyebrow at him. "I also know you have vodka stashed underneath the counter, so why don't you be a pal and bring it out."

Phil grinned and pulled out the bottle. No one could say no to Lorelei—not even a former heavyweight boxer who still weighed upwards of 220 pounds.

"Is the Piping Plover going to be okay?" I managed to ask Sam.

"The roof's fine on the west side," she said. "I can run the shop out of half the space if I need to. But we're at the end of tourist season anyway. How many LIFE'S A BEACH shirts am I going to sell?"

Lorelei said, "We got a little flooded, but everything's fine. What happened to you, Anne?"

I waited until our Bloody Marys were delivered and I took a sip. Maybe it was the state of shock I was in, but I felt lightheaded almost immediately. "I basically have half of a house left," I said.

"Which half?" Lorelei asked immediately.

"The darkroom's gone."

They both gasped. "Oh, Annie," Sam said.

I tried to shrug. Tried to sound...undevastated. *Was that even a word?* I told them what had happened, and then I attempted a brave smile. "I never cooked much, so the kitchen can go."

"*That's* the glass half full," Sam said.

"And...maybe I need to take a break from wedding and pet photography."

"But you do more than that," Lorelei protested. "You were going to have that show—"

I interrupted her. "Just because the gallerist said he liked my photos doesn't mean he was going to give me a solo show. Anyway, brides and dogs paid the mortgage. Not my art photography." I put my face in my hands.

"We'll help you get back on your feet," Lorelei said gently. "Everything's going to be okay. Seriously. Someday this'll be just another story you'll tell."

"Everybody has a storm story," Sam added. "Do you have any idea how many times my dad told about the time he went fishing during Tropical Storm Charlie, got swept off his boat, and spent twenty-nine hours in the ocean, clinging to a cooler? When the Coast Guard finally rescued him, the first thing he did was open that cooler, crack a Budweiser, and ask those heroes if they had any chips."

"He dined out on that story for years," Lorelei said, rolling her eyes.

I laughed, despite myself. "I guess some people just know what they want," I said. "I wish my problems felt so simple."

"Well what do you truly need, hon, besides a new roof over your head and a bit of insurance money?" Lorelei asked.

I thought for a moment. I'd come here to make a fresh start after my divorce—and I *had*. But it took only one single night to wipe it all out. "I think I need to get away for a little while," I said.

Lorelei frowned. "Anne," she said, "you need to stay and deal."

I shook my head. "I'll put Bill in charge. He's dealt with hurricane damage before."

"You can't just leave your house half wrecked," Sam said.

But why not? I certainly couldn't *live* in it. And the more they tried to persuade me that it was crucial I stick around, the more certain I was that I'd be leaving in the morning.

"My couch is your couch," Sam was saying. "And Lorelei's got a spare bedroom."

"You guys really are the best," I said.

"So you'll stay?"

I smiled again, and this time I felt what might have been a tiny sliver of hope. "I've got other plans," I said.

Chapter 4

*A*LL RIGHT, so calling them "plans" was something of a stretch. I'd decided to go visit my brother in Roanoke, but after that? I didn't know. I figured I'd see where the winds took me. I'd just hope they wouldn't be gale force, because I'd had enough of those.

By some miracle, my car—a formerly gorgeous vintage Mercedes I'd named Beatrice, now salt-streaked and rusted—still ran.

I quickly loaded it with things I'd need for the trip: inland clothes (no flip-flops, no baggy beach dresses), a few slightly soggy books I'd been meaning to read, and my laptop and phone. Though it wasn't particularly practical, I took my spider plant from its place on the windowsill and set it on the front seat. I'd had it since I was a freshman in college, and it seemed cruel to leave it behind. It was the closest thing I had to a pet.

"I guess you'll be riding shotgun," I said, and then I laughed a little crazily because I was talking to a plant.

I grabbed a red coral cameo that had belonged to my mother, and a little jar of fossilized sharks' teeth that I'd found on my beach. I'd moved around a lot since college—from New York City to Long Island, and then to Boston, then Raleigh—but this tiny little North Carolina island was the first place that had felt like home.

While I gathered my things, I tried to keep my eyes fixed on the intact part of my house. But right before I was ready to go, I let myself creep toward the remains of the darkroom, which I'd built myself. The shelves were broken, the enlarger crushed, and the bottles of developer and stabilizer spilled onto the ruined floor.

The question was: If *that* was gone, what, really, was worth saving?

When I went back outside, Bill was standing in the driveway with three cans of motor oil, a first-aid kit, and a tuna sandwich from Zell's Café. "Thought you could use these," he said.

I took them gratefully. "You're sure you don't mind?" I said. "Overseeing the...whatever?" I gestured toward the house. Whether it'd be patched back up or torn down entirely was an open question, and the insurance company was in charge of the answer.

"Course not," he said. "What else do I have to do? Can't run the charters when the tourists aren't here."

I reached out and pulled him to me in a hard hug. He was surprised, obviously, but eventually he sort of hugged me back.

"You be careful," he said.

"I will," I promised.

"Maybe you want to take this," he said. And then he

handed me my beloved Nikon, its lens missing and its body gritty with sand. "I found it underneath my house."

I took the camera from him gently, as if it were alive but gravely wounded.

"Thank you," I said. "For everything."

And then I got in my car and drove away.

Chapter 5

I HADN'T seen my brother, Ben, in three years — not since our dad's funeral. But after only five hours of driving, there I was, standing on his front porch, wondering why I hadn't made the trip sooner.

When I knocked, the door flew open and a giant Labrador came barreling out, nearly knocking me back down the steps. Ben stood in the hall, grinning and shaking his head. "Sorry about Stanley," he said. "He's sweet, but he's crazier than a squirrel on speed."

The dog was now racing around the yard in ecstatic circles. "No kidding," I said laughing and stepped inside.

I followed Ben into his cozy kitchen and sat down at the same pinewood table we'd eaten dinner around when we were kids. He brought us each a beer.

"It's so good to see you," we said simultaneously. Then, quick as we could, "JinxyouowemeaCoke."

Ben clinked my glass with his. "Cheers, big sis," he said. And then, "I'm really sorry about . . . Claire."

"Both of them, right?" I asked wryly. Until I could

make those two disasters into a good story, they could at least be a punch line.

"You know you can stay here for a while if you want," he said.

"I know—thank you. But I'm going to do some traveling."

Then I explained what I'd realized on the drive up: After Patrick left, I'd moved to Topsail Island and basically gone into hiding. Even before that, I'd lost touch with a lot of people—which was a problem. "Take Karen Landey," I said. "She was my best friend for *sixteen years,* and now I see her only on Instagram. So sure, I know what she ate for dinner last night—but I haven't met her baby."

"Um, didn't she have that baby five years ago?" Ben asked.

"My point exactly," I cried. "It's time to go see a few old friends."

Ben nodded thoughtfully. "Have you mentioned that to them?"

"Not yet," I admitted. "But cut me some slack, I only figured it out an hour ago. I'll write Karen tonight."

He laughed. "It's a great idea. Take pictures, okay?"

My shoulders immediately slumped.

Without saying anything, Ben got up and walked down the hall, and when he returned he set two boxes in front of me. "It's a Nikon D5300 DSLR with a portable photo printer. I bought them for you last Christmas—"

"Oh no!" I interrupted, horrified. "That was when I

told you I'd rather cut off an arm than go digital. I'm so sorry! I had no idea!"

Ben shrugged. "No big deal. But maybe you can use this stuff now." Then he snorted. "Annie, stop looking at it like it's going to bite you."

"I'm not — It's just . . ."

"It's like giving a girl who's only ever ridden a donkey the keys to a Ferrari?" he asked.

I laughed. "I'm going to try not to take that as an insult. And thank you. I'll . . . I'll try these out. Really, I will."

He got up again. "You hungry? I made spaghetti. Homemade sauce, noodles, everything."

"Considering I'm barely past opening cans of Spa-ghettiOs, that sounds amazing."

The dinner was even better than I expected: San Marzanos in a buttery sauce over hand-cut tagliatelle, and a kale Caesar so good it nearly brought tears to my eyes. I was helping myself to round two when Ben caught sight of the coral cameo, hanging on a thin gold chain around my neck.

"Where'd you get that?" he asked.

"It was Mom's," I said. "Isn't it beautiful? Dad gave it to her."

Ben held out his hand and I put the necklace into his big palm. He turned the cameo over and back.

"What?" I asked. "You have a funny look on your face."

"Dad might have given it to her. But he didn't buy it for her."

I set my fork down. "What do you mean?"

"He bought it for Kathy Pasters. But Mom found it in his sock drawer, and she assumed it was for her," Ben said.

"*Excuse* me?"

Ben looked at me in surprise. "You really didn't know? Dad and Kit were a thing for a while."

I couldn't believe it. I had no idea what to say. "Mom and Dad, Kit and Joe—they all used to play euchre together," I cried.

"Yeah, and Dad and Kit were playing footsie under the table." He ripped a piece of garlic bread in two. "Everybody has secrets, Annie," he said. "You were just probably too busy messing around with your camera to notice what Dad's was."

Suddenly I felt confused and sad. Was I really so blind? This new story of my parents' marriage wasn't the one I wanted to be true.

"But I think, in the end, they were happy," Ben added, as if he could read my mind. "I really do."

Okay, maybe, I thought—because I wanted him to be right. *But how did their marriage survive an affair when mine went belly-up?*

The world was full of mysteries.

I wondered if Patrick Quinn could help me solve that particular one. Had we made the right choice? Were we, in the end, happy—apart?

Ben hoisted steaming strands of spaghetti with a pair of silver tongs that also used to belong to our parents. "Thirds?" he asked.

I shook my head. "No thanks." I wasn't hungry anymore. I was busy calculating how long it would take to get to my ex-husband's house.

Chapter 6

BETTER person might have warned him—I know. But this wasn't going to be an emotional ambush. As the saying goes, I came in peace.

I called Patrick from the historic main drag of Ellicott City, an affluent town just outside of Baltimore. "I'm across the street from a place called Renard—is that French for fox? Duck? I forget. Anyway, would you like to meet me there for dinner?" I asked.

"Anne? Wow—uh, *hi*," Patrick stammered. He'd never been the world's most articulate person. "Yes. I mean, of course. It's ... really good to hear your voice."

"I'll see you in twenty," I said, exhibiting a firmness I never had in our marriage.

I ordered a bottle of sparkling wine while I waited at a window table, watching people pass by outside. A little girl stopped and waved to me, and I waved back, noting her darling smile and her obviously DIY haircut.

I wondered if her mother had committed that crime against her bangs or if that pixie had sneaked into the bathroom with a pair of scissors. Probably there was a funny story about it.

As a photographer, I'd spent so much time focusing (no pun intended) on people's looks: on the way a bride squinted in direct sunlight or how a groom's boutonnière complemented his bowtie.

But what if I started really paying attention to people's *words?*

It had begun to seem like everybody had an incredible story—whether or not it was happy or if they ever even wanted to tell it.

And here I was, revisiting the plot of Patrick's and mine.

What if I could collect those stories—into some kind of a book? It was a crazy idea. But then again, so was moving to an island I'd only been to once before. And that had worked out beautifully.

At least it had until two days ago.

I was busy contemplating this possible new project when Patrick breezed into the restaurant, wearing a slightly rumpled shirt and a pair of obviously expensive blue jeans. I felt the same flutter of nerves I had when I first met him near the 79th Street entrance to Central Park.

"You look beautiful," he said as he sat down across from me. His eyes were as blue as ever.

"Flatterer," I said. My smile was genuine. I really *was* happy to see him, despite everything. Honestly, this surprised me a little.

"What in the world brings you to E.C.?" he asked.

I poured some brut into Patrick's glass. "You," I said simply.

He looked slightly alarmed, and I couldn't help laughing.

"I'm not here to ask for you back if that's what you're worried about," I assured him.

He ducked his head. "I wasn't *worried*," he said.

I shrugged. "I think I just want to know what happened. I mean, besides the obvious."

The obvious was that I'd found another woman's underpants in the laundry, mixed in with the towels. They weren't hot pink satin or crotchless lace — nothing dramatic like that. Their only distinguishing feature was that they *weren't mine*.

Patrick gazed into his wine. "I guess I got scared," he said finally. "About what marriage meant."

"You mean the bit about until death do us part?" I asked.

He nodded. "Yeah, I guess."

"Aha," I said. "So instead of death, it was Claire's panties."

He flushed and nodded again, almost imperceptibly this time.

I leaned forward. "Do you think you were the only one who was scared? Did you think it was easy for me, standing up in front of all those people in that church and basically saying 'I, Anne McWilliams, have been wrong about many, many things in my life, but this one thing I am *not* wrong about'?"

"I don't know," he said. "Probably not."

"How is Claire, by the way?" I asked—not that I particularly cared.

"You'd have to ask her," he said. "She's in Atlanta now."

Well, *that* was interesting news.

Patrick leaned forward. "You know what, though, Anne? You're up there on your high horse like *I'm* the one who screwed everything up. But you have some responsibility here, too. You could have been willing to try to work it out. I wanted to, remember? But you wouldn't do it. You just left." He shrugged. "You think I'm the one who threw everything away," he said quietly. "But maybe that distinction belongs to you."

I sucked in my breath sharply. This was a new interpretation of events. And maybe, just maybe, there was some truth in it.

What if, in the end, *I'd* been the one who was truly scared of commitment? And how had I never figured that out before? I just didn't know what to say.

"I have something to show you," Patrick said. He pulled out his wallet, dug around in it, and then extracted a small envelope, which he placed on the table between us.

When I opened it, I saw the engagement ring he'd given me, with its rose-gold band and its bright, tiny diamond. I'd wanted a ring from him so badly.

Or at least I'd thought I had.

"Are you giving this back?" I whispered.

"No. I assumed when you threw it out the window

and into the yard that you didn't want it anymore. I just wanted to show you that"—he stopped and shook his head, as if he needed to clear it—"that I carry it around. That it still means something to me." He looked up at me. "And so do you." He reached for my hand. "I made some mistakes," he said.

No kidding, I thought. But then again, I'd clearly made some, too.

"We all do," I said.

"I'm sorry," he said.

"Me too."

As I held Patrick's warm hand, I suddenly seemed to remember everything: the surprise snow on our wedding day, the epic dinner parties we hosted, the crazy road trip to Glacier National Park, how he sang "Hey Jude" when he shaved, the way he always put his arm around my shoulders as we walked.

What if I could have it all back, just like that?

It was so very tempting.

But it wouldn't work, I knew it. We were too different, too stubborn—maybe even too damaged. But, I hoped, we were on our way toward healing.

Patrick's fingers gently stroked mine. "So what do we do now?" he asked quietly.

I smiled at him. "We order dinner," I said.

"And then?"

"We kiss each other sweetly," I said. "And then we go our separate ways."

This was how a lovely French meal became the epilogue to the story of Patrick Quinn and Anne McWilliams.

They might live happily ever after, I could write, *just not with each other.*

Chapter 7

*T*HE FIRST pictures I took on my digital camera were of my ex-husband as he walked away down the lamp-lit street, under the green boughs of an elm tree. It felt achingly sad, but somehow fitting, too — a way of closing one door and opening another.

But what that new door led to — besides no longer living in the photographic dark ages — well, I didn't really know. I had no job and no home, and not very many prospects, either. On the bright side, though, I had a credit card and a book idea. Was that enough to carry me forward?

Tomorrow I'd start driving to Iowa City, where my best friend, Karen Landey, lived with her husband and the daughter I'd never met. It was nearly fourteen hours away, and Karen had told me to hop on the next flight. But I had Beatrice, my plant, and way too much luggage to stuff in a 737 overhead compartment.

I told her I wanted to take the slow route anyway, though, because of my crazy new idea. Seatmates notwithstanding, it's hard to gather stories when you're soaring thirty-five thousand feet above anyone who might tell you one.

After a good night's sleep on a cushy feathertop in an overpriced Ellicott City inn, I bought the world's biggest coffee and hit I-70. I cranked the radio up as loud as it could go and opened all the windows to let in the late August air. With my big black sunglasses and bright red lipstick, I felt freer than I had in ages.

When, sixty miles up the road, a Neko Case song came on the radio, I sang along like I was trying out for *The Voice*. "Let this be a warning says the magpie to the morning. Don't let this fading summer pass you by."

I didn't care that Beatrice could barely hit sixty-five miles per hour without overheating. I had *time*. The weight of my failed marriage had lifted and so had my spirits. In the rushing wind, my spider plant's leaves were like green fingers, waving: *Adios amigos!*

"I will not let this fading summer pass me by, Spidey," I said, and I didn't even feel stupid for talking to the thing.

I was so happy that I didn't notice my speedometer had crept up to nearly eighty. I didn't notice the trucker motioning me to pull over. But I did hear the deep, bellowing honk of his horn. And I couldn't miss the smoke that suddenly came pouring out from my hood.

Chapter 8

THE KID waiting by the fuel island at Atomic Gas and Auto took one look at my overheated car and ran off like he thought it might explode.

I grabbed my bag and plant and hustled to safety myself. A moment later, a man with close-cropped dark hair and high cheekbones, wearing a blue grease-stained jumpsuit, walked leisurely over to my car.

He waved away the billowing smoke. "You can stop hiding behind the trash can," he said. "She's not going to blow up."

I wondered how he knew Beatrice was a she. I crept over, not entirely sure I could trust him about a potential explosion. The air smelled like gas and burned plastic.

He looked over his shoulder at the kid, who didn't seem like he believed him either. "Taylor," he called, "I need you to finish up on that oil change I was working on."

The man—Josh, his name tag said—touched Beatrice's hood thoughtfully. "This is a 1977 W123s, isn't it."

It wasn't a question. I nodded.

"I was afraid of that," he said. Then he popped open the hood and disappeared into the smoke.

"Why?" I asked. I could hear the panic in my voice.

"You've got a plastic radiator in here. Those things are famous for upper radiator neck failure." He shut the hood and stood up again. "I'm guessing you've lost all your coolant and your aluminum core's probably damaged. That means you're looking at a replacement."

I sucked in my breath. "The whole radiator?"

He grimaced in a way I could tell was meant to be sympathetic. "Or maybe the whole car," he said.

And I felt, suddenly, as if I was disintegrating. If Beatrice was gone, then what? She was basically the only thing I had left.

I sank down to the curb and sat with my head cradled in my hands.

The mechanic put his hand on my shoulder. "I'm sorry, miss," he said. "But you're lucky, you know. If that radiator neck had popped all the way off, you might not even be here right now."

I looked up at him. "I'm lucky I didn't die, huh? That is seriously *bottom-of-the-barrel* luck," I said.

He gave me a half smile. "Or else it's the best kind of luck there is. It depends on how you look at it. Your personal philosophy, if you will."

"What is this, *Zen and the Art of Mercedes Maintenance*?" I muttered.

The mechanic offered me his hand and pulled me up to standing.

"Let me get her into the bay and take a closer look," he said. "Zelda's is a good place to have a bite while you're waiting."

I turned in the direction he was pointing. Five hundred yards off, I could see a low white building, and then nothing but fields and trees for miles. Zelda's was obviously the *only* place to get something to eat. "Okay," I said weakly. "See you in—"

"An hour," he said.

Inside the diner, a pretty red-haired waitress poured a coffee for me before I'd even sat down.

"You look like you could use it," she said. "You all right?"

I shrugged. Was I? "My car might be a . . ." I waved my arm toward the garage. I couldn't say the word *goner,* but that's what I was thinking.

"Well if anyone can fix it, Josh can," she said reassuringly. "He's like an engine Einstein."

I took a sip of the coffee. It wasn't great, but at least it was strong. "I take it you know him."

"We went to school together," she said.

"Were you friends?" I asked, hoping conversation would keep me from complete despair.

She laughed. "We were more than friends," she said. She pulled a cloth from the pocket of her apron and began wiping the counter. "But he was more than friends with a lot of girls."

"Funny, I had a husband like that," I said. My smile probably looked a bit grim.

She refilled my coffee though I'd only taken a couple of sips. And then, because I was the only customer, she sat down on a stool next to me. "You want to talk about it?" she asked.

"Not really," I said. "You know, water under the bridge and all."

"Some of my customers really like to talk," she said. "You'd think I was their therapist, not their waitress."

"You must hear good stories," I said.

"Sure," she said. "Good ones, bad ones — mostly boring ones, honestly. 'No, Mr. Scharf, I don't need a blow-by-blow account of you passing a kidney stone,' you know?"

I laughed. "In fairness to Mr. Scharf, whoever he is, that story sounds more disgusting than boring."

"True," she admitted.

"So what's your story?" I asked.

She looked quizzically at me. "What do you mean?"

"Like, what would you tell *your* therapist-waitress?" I asked.

She smiled then, and it just lit up her whole face. "Okay, I'll tell you something," she said. "Ten years ago I was a knockout. Hell, even five years ago I was still pretty hot." She held up a warning hand. "Don't bother telling me I still look great."

"I was going to," I admitted.

"So one day I won a makeover contest — you know, you mail in your picture, and the TV producers pick you to be on their show. So here I am, Kate Prior, the small-town waitress, getting flown to Los Angeles. They gave me hand-painted blond highlights and put so much makeup on my face it felt like spackling paste. When I walked out on stage, the women in the audience clapped and screamed. Suddenly I looked like Miss America! It was *wild*." She shook her head and chuckled at the memory. "Later they took me to a really fancy party. I had agents in expensive suits on either side of me, pouring me Champagne and trying to sign me. They said they could build my brand, make me a household name. And I'm like, 'Brand? What does that mean? I'm not a laundry detergent!' But at the same time it was wonderful. You should have seen the shoes they gave me—they cost more than my car."

"Mine, too, no doubt," I said, and I felt a pang of sorrow for Beatrice.

Kate reached into a case and got us each a croissant. I'd never been in a restaurant where people just *handed* you things.

"So later I'm chatting with this great lady—she's a movie producer—and some hot guy she's with," Kate went on. "And she says to him, 'I want to get a picture with Kate.' So I go to put my arm around her, and I'm smiling all big and proud, but then she gives *me* the camera. This was before selfies, so I'm really confused—until I turn around, and I see *Kate Winslet* right behind me. The producer doesn't want a picture of me! She wants a picture of *herself with Kate Winslet*. And Kate Winslet knows this, and she's laughing her British ass off.

But I roll with it. I go, 'One Kate at a time—get in line behind me, Limey.' Even though, inside, I was dying."

My mouth had fallen open. "And then what?" I asked.

Kate shrugged. "I went back to my hotel room, and my daughter was so freaked out by my new look that she hid under the bed." She started laughing. "She wouldn't come out until I washed off all my makeup and changed into my ratty old pj's."

"And *then* what happened," I said.

"And then I flew home and came back to work at Zelda's," she said, shrugging. "By the way, do you want to hear about today's specials?"

Later, when I asked if I could take her picture, Kate posed with one hand on her hip and the other on the handle of a coffee pot. Her smile was dazzling.

"Do you ever wish—," I began.

Kate cut me off. "I wish a lot of things," she said. She gazed out the diner window at the flat fields stretching far away. "But girl, I don't wish I'd tried to become a brand. I'd rather be a real person, and a good mother. Like I believe I am." Then she turned to me and grinned. "I do wish I still had those shoes, though."

Chapter 9

I FELT a little better walking back to the gas station, and when Josh the mechanic came out to meet me with a smile on his face, I felt my spirits lift even higher.

"How's Beatrice?" I asked eagerly.

"I can fix her in half a day," he said.

"That's amazing," I cried.

"But the parts are going to take two weeks to get here," he said, "and they're going to cost an arm, a leg, and a kidney."

The balloon of my happiness instantly popped. "You're supposed to tell me that *first*," I said. "To not get my hopes up."

"I'm sorry," he said. "I try to focus on the positive."

We walked into the service station waiting area and I sat down on one of the vinyl chairs. Despite all the coffee, I felt exhausted.

Josh took a seat across from me. "I'm guessing you don't want to wait. And that maybe you don't need to spend a few thousand dollars on a car that" — he looked out the window at her — "that probably has two tires in the junkyard already."

"Be gentle," I cried. "That's my life companion you're talking about."

"I'm not telling you to junk her. I'm just saying…"

"That I need a new car?"

Josh leaned forward and clasped his hands together, his expression earnest. "I get the sense you're trying to go somewhere kind of far away. And I just don't think she'll be the lady to take you."

I paused to let this sad news sink in. "So you've got a sweet ride you want to sell me?" I asked eventually — and skeptically.

He smiled. "I don't know if I'd go that far. But I do have something that'll get you where you're going. Do you want to take a look?"

I didn't, actually, but I was desperate, so I followed him around back of the garage. I just couldn't wait two weeks for a repair.

Maybe this was a lesson for me: *There's always more to lose.*

There were half a dozen cars parked in a small lot behind the shop, and most of them looked like they wouldn't even turn on, let alone drive eight hundred miles.

"Really?" I said to Josh.

"Over here," he said. Then he pointed to a small black van with a purple stripe along the side, and a bumper sticker that read MY OTHER CAR IS THE MILLENNIUM FALCON.

"You've got to be kidding me," I said.

"Only sixty-five thousand miles," he said.

"And it's cheap because it's incredibly ugly?" I asked hopefully.

He laughed. "I think it's a bargain. It'll run for another ten years at least."

I hope I don't need it that long, I thought. "You think you're going to cruise around in a Mercedes — and you end up in a minivan," I said softly.

"Everything changes. Nothing remains without change," Josh said, equally quietly.

"And now you're going to quote *Buddha,*" I said, shaking my head. But at the same time, it made me feel better. "Promise to take good care of Beatrice," I said. "Don't put her back here with these losers."

"I won't," he said.

"I'll come back for her," I said. *I hope.*

As I signed the paperwork to buy the van, a hollow ache in my guts, I asked, "Do you have a good story?"

Josh looked confused. "What do you mean?"

"I mean — is there some funny thing you like to tell people? Or something not funny. Whatever. Just a really good story."

He gazed up at the ceiling fan, turning slowly in the August heat. Then he smiled at me, almost mischievously. "Once upon a time," he said, "there was a great mechanic. He was a happy guy. He had a nice house, a good truck, and a better dog. And then one day, a beautiful, dark-haired stranger came into his repair shop."

I felt my cheeks flush. "Are you—"

He held up a hand. "Wait for it! Her car was a disaster—not even he, engine expert that he was, could fix it that day. But she didn't really mind, because he was so handsome and charming. And when he asked her out on a date, she said yes."

"And then?" I said. By now my cheeks were on fire.

"And then they had the best date of their lives," he said.

"Wow," I managed.

"And so then they had another amazing date. And not long after *that* date, he proposed. And she said yes again." His smile was electric now.

And me? I didn't know whether to be flattered or alarmed.

He leaned forward. "Do you want to see her picture?"

Finally, the truth dawned on me. "Oh my God," I said. "What?"

"It really happened! I thought you were making it up," I admitted, laughing. "I thought it was about *us*."

He laughed, too. "You're beautiful, it's true," he said. "But I'm married. I just don't wear the ring because I don't like it getting greasy."

Still laughing, I asked him to pose for a picture next to Beatrice. He said yes.

That way I could remember them both.

Chapter 10

BY THE time I pulled into the Starlight Motor Inn in Richmond, Indiana, I was farther west than I'd ever been before. (How a person could get to age thirty-six without crossing the Mississippi—I didn't know, but I'd soon be able to cross that off my list.)

My room was tiny, but nicer than the motel's flickering neon sign had led me to expect, with pale gray walls, a cute mini-kitchen, and a vase of fresh daisies on the dresser. I took a long hot shower, washing off the grit of the road, and lay down to close my eyes for a minute. The next thing I knew, I was being torn from the warm arms of sleep by the sound of my neighbors having loud, yowling sex.

Or else maybe the Starlight kept a roomful of feral cats next door—I couldn't be sure. I looked at my watch. It was ten o'clock.

Disoriented and starving, I gathered loose change from various pockets and headed to the vending machines outside the motel office, where I bought myself Cheetos, Snickers, and a Diet Coke. I'd never been much of a cook, but this was taking not cooking to a whole new level.

Welcome to life on the road, I thought giddily, and bit into the Snickers. *If only the vending machine sold earplugs, too.*

The small motel pool glowed turquoise in the darkness, and so instead of going back to my room, I opened the creaky gate, slipped off my shoes, and dunked my bare feet into the cool water.

I washed down the Snickers with the soda and congratulated myself on getting this far on my solo journey. Obviously my circumstances weren't glamorous — but I was having an *adventure*. And wasn't that worth something?

As I sat there, reflecting, the rush of cars passing by on the highway began to remind me of the sound of the ocean. Soon I was overcome with longing for my island, my beach, my house — for all the things I didn't have anymore.

I wondered what Josh the philosopher-mechanic would say to make me feel better: *At least your van runs well,* maybe, and something about how I ought to *make something good out of something bad*.

Easy for him to say.

But in a way, I *was* making something good — or at least I was trying to. I'd already gathered a handful of stories and photographs, and I was on my way to gather more. Maybe, just maybe, something would come of them.

The gate creaked open then, and a woman came inside the pool area. She was wrapped in a blanket and bleary-eyed, her hair mussed. She sat down on one of the deck lounge chairs and heaved a big sigh.

I ignored her, in case she was one of the people I'd just heard going at it. TMI, you know?

But eventually she spoke. In a smoker's voice, she asked, "Are you married?"

"No," I said, leaving it at that.

"Good. Let me give you a piece of advice. Do not, under any circumstances, marry a man who snores."

I laughed in surprise. "I have a history of not taking good advice. But that sounds reasonable."

"It's more than reasonable," she said. "It's crucial."

"Like a deal breaker?" I said.

She looked at me as if I were crazy. "Of course! Do you think I want to be out here in the middle of the night on a lounge chair by some crappy pool, talking to some sad-looking lady?"

"I guess not," I said. Thinking: *Do I really look sad?*

"I get no peace," she said.

She was quiet for a while then. And in the darkness, by an anonymous motel and beside a total stranger, I felt more alone than I'd ever felt.

But it wasn't sad. It just *was.*

When I looked over at her next, she was asleep.

And a few minutes later, she started to snore.

Welcome to life on the road.

Chapter 11

KAREN'S HOUSE was large and gracious, with a carefully landscaped yard and a gleaming Volvo parked in the driveway. As I climbed out of my ugly van, brushing crumbs from my clothes, I felt rumpled and underdressed.

It wasn't an unfamiliar feeling. My friendship with Karen had always seemed unlikely to me, like one of those cross-species bonds people make videos about: a gazelle becoming best friends with a tortoise, for example.

Quick, beautiful, magnetic Karen—the gazelle, obviously—was now standing in the doorway, motioning me inside her *Better Homes and Gardens* Victorian.

"Hurry!" she called. "Sophie gets home from kindergarten in an hour and I've got news that she can't hear."

We hugged each other hard. "Really, she's old enough for school already?"

Karen smiled. "I can't believe it either. Come in, come in. Do you want to shower and change?"

I surreptitiously sniffed an armpit. "Do I need to?"

"No." She laughed. "I was just trying to be hospitable. You look—and smell—perfect."

"Well, I wouldn't go *that* far," I said.

She led me through the house and onto the screened-in back porch, where she got us each a seltzer from a silver ice bucket. "Six *years* since I've seen you. How can that be?" she asked, settling into a wicker rocking chair.

"It's terrible, I know," I said. "But I'm so happy to see you now. You look exactly the same."

"Well, if you add fifteen pounds," she said lightly. Then her tone changed. "I'm so sorry about your house."

I waved this away. "Let's not talk about it. I've decided my coping strategy is denial."

Karen folded her long legs beneath her and leaned back in her chair. "All right then. Maybe you want the dirt on our old classmates."

She'd always been a fount of social knowledge, and I its willing recipient. "Of course," I said.

"Leah Larsen got divorced, for one thing."

"It happens to the best of us," I said wryly.

"Absolutely. So then her husband took up with the neighbor after Leah left him, which basically started a chain reaction of divorces in the ol' hometown. Dan Smith—you remember him, right?—is in jail for marijuana possession, and his ex, Dodie Scheffer, is running for mayor and no one even finds that ironic. Jennifer Meyers and Jacob Sales finally got together after years of secret, seemingly unrequited love for each other, and they spent the summer following Eagles of Death Metal around on tour."

I laughed. "It amazes me how you *still* know what's going on with everyone."

"Some people stay in touch when they move away," she said—a bit pointedly, I thought.

"But I wasn't friends with all those people," I said. "You were."

"Well you could have been," she said. "Instead you were always disappearing into the darkroom. The rest of us were living in the actual world—and you were living in what you could see through your camera's viewfinder."

I sighed. "I'm coming to realize that."

She smiled. "It's nothing to regret. We are who we are."

"Well, I am trying to branch out a little," I said. "I told you about my book project."

"Your best story," Karen said, nodding thoughtfully. "Like the time we stole all the lawn ornaments from Bob Ubbin's yard? Or maybe when we went hot-tubbing in January and then got pneumonia at the same time and missed the winter formal?"

"Right, which would have sucked anyway," I said, laughing. "Those are funny anecdotes—but they're not a *best* story."

Karen looked out over her pretty lawn and shook her head. "No, I guess not," she said. "The answer's easy, though. Sophie's my best story."

I could hear the love and awe in her voice. But Sophie

wasn't a story; she was a person. "Sorry—narratively unsatisfying," I said, nudging Karen playfully.

"I could tell you about giving birth. *That's* a story."

"Well…"

"Yeah, you probably don't want to hear it. It's rather gruesome. All right, let me think." She frowned lightly. "But Anne, you already know all my stories. You're *in* them."

"Tell me a secret, then," I said.

Karen looked down at her hands for a moment, and then she looked up at me. "All right," she said. She took a deep breath. "Do you remember that beautiful velvet dress you had in college?"

"That slate-blue one?" I asked. "I *loved* that dress. But then one day it just vanished. I always wondered what happened to it."

Karen bit her lip, then spoke. "I'm about to tell you," she said.

Chapter 12

I FELT a jolt of surprise. "Oh. Okay."

"You'd gone home to see your dad for his birthday. There was a dance that weekend, and I didn't have anything to wear, so I went into your closet and there it was. I knew it was the prettiest thing you owned. I knew you'd bought it with your own money and that you wouldn't really want me to borrow it. But I also knew that if I asked, you would have said yes. So I took it. And I wore it to the dance." She glanced over at me and seemed to wince a little. "But the problem was I got drunk. Really drunk. And halfway through the dance, I threw up all over it."

"My beautiful dress," I half whispered.

She nodded. "I took it to cleaners all over town, but it was utterly ruined. So for a while it lived in a paper bag under my bed. And then one day I threw it in a Dumpster behind the dining hall."

"And you never said a thing!" I said, shocked. I was kind of mad, too. What a stupid, mean secret to keep!

But then a memory flickered in my mind. It was dim at first, and then it grew bright and clear. "Wait a second," I said. "That was the spring of the magic money, wasn't it?"

All that spring I'd kept finding cash—five dollars here, ten there—in the pockets of my jeans or crumpled at the bottom of my messy backpack. Once a twenty appeared in my makeup bag. When I told Karen about these exciting discoveries, she'd brushed them off. "You've never been able to keep track of anything, Anne," she'd pointed out. "Why on earth would your money be any different?"

But now I finally understood. "*You* were hiding all that money in my stuff!" I said.

"I was trying to pay you back," Karen admitted.

"I can't believe it," I said. "Is that why you took that second work study job?

She nodded again. "I swear, I've felt bad about it for fifteen years."

I leaned forward and put my hand on her knee. The flare of anger I'd felt had vanished. "Honey," I said. "When my mother was dying, you *moved into my house.* You slept on the floor of my bedroom for most of our senior year in high school because I couldn't bear to be alone. My whole *life* I've been able to count on you." I felt tears prick at the corners of my eyes. "You've always been there. You can throw up on every single thing I own, and I'll still love you forever."

Now I thought Karen looked like she might cry, too. "That's good," she said quietly. "Because actually I *might* throw up." She smiled. "You see, I'm pregnant. And it's twins. That's what I wanted to tell you."

I just about fell out of my chair. But when I'd recovered from the surprise, I hugged her tightly. "Oh my God, I'm so happy for you."

"Me, too," she said. "I think," she added. Then she got up and motioned me to follow. "Perfect timing — I hear the school bus."

Out front, we watched a dozen kids dash off the bus, and then one small blond girl came running toward us. She practically leaped into Karen's arms, and as she clung to her mother, her words came out in a rush. "Mommy I read all of *Are You My Mother?* today out loud and I'm starving and can I have a playdate with Clara because she got a guinea pig and will we have dessert tonight or is it a night I only get fruit and how many days is it until my birthday?"

Karen laughed and kissed her on both cheeks, then gently set her down. "Before I tackle those questions, let me introduce you to my oldest, bestest friend, Anne."

I knelt down and gazed into the bright green eyes of Karen's best story. "I've wanted to meet you for *years,*" I said, smiling at her. She was tiny and perfect and beautiful, with dirty knees and a smudge of spaghetti sauce on her face. "Would it be okay if I gave you just a little hug?"

She nodded, and so I took her into my arms. She giggled, wriggly as a fish, and I marveled at the loveliness of her small body. *It's true what they say,* I thought. *Life really is a miracle.*

She whispered, "It's nice to meet you. Please stay for dinner. That way we'll have dessert."

Chapter 13

KAREN INSISTED we go out that evening—for old times' sake. "You're going to like this place," she promised as she led me to the door of the Gooseneck Tavern.

"I don't want to drink alone," I protested.

"Trust me, you're not going to."

"Can't we just keep sitting on your porch—"

She shoved me gently toward the entrance. "Didn't you say you were trying to expand your horizons? Here's your chance to prove it."

Inside the tavern, Christmas lights suspended from low rafters bathed everything in a rosy glow. A band played on a small stage at the far end of the room, and over the din of chatter, I could hear the strains of a twangy, acoustic version of "Dead Flowers."

"I can't believe I'm out on a school night," Karen said giddily. "With eye shadow on and everything."

"You're living *la vida loca*," I agreed.

"In *Iowa* City, *Iowa*," she added. "It truly boggles the mind."

At the bar I ordered a gin and tonic for me, and a club

soda for the mother-to-be. I still couldn't believe Karen's news. But I was thrilled for her, I really was. In another six months, she'd have three children sitting in the back of her shining Volvo.

And me—well, I'd have a van and a spider plant.

I guess I wasn't quite sure how to feel about that.

"Maybe we should find you a little fling tonight," Karen suggested, leaning back against the bar and scanning the room.

"Look at me," I said. "I'm wearing old jeans and an even older T-shirt." I glanced down at my Frye booties. "My shoe game is on point, though."

Karen sighed. "When are you going to stop pretending like you're not gorgeous, Anne?"

"Says Malibu Barbie," I muttered.

She elbowed me. "I heard that."

"I haven't been on a date since I left Patrick," I admitted. "You know, the guy you told me I shouldn't marry," I added, because I couldn't help reminding her.

"Well, was I wrong?" she asked.

"We had a little over two good years."

"And one terrible one."

"Just because something doesn't work out in the end doesn't mean it was bad from the beginning. I'm not sorry for it," I said.

She nodded. "Good. You shouldn't be. That which doesn't kill you—"

"I hate it when people say that!"

"I know. That's why I said it." She smiled wistfully.

"Don't think I don't sometimes wish I could run away to Aruba the way you ran off to that island."

"North Carolina is hardly Aruba."

"Well it ain't Iowa, either."

"Touché," I said.

She put her arm around my shoulders. "Want to go check out the band with your old best pal?"

We wound our way through the crowd and found places in front of the stage. I noted the lead singer—a young woman with bleached, spiky hair—and the old guy on the pedal steel, and the bearded giant manhandling a stand-up bass. But my eyes were quickly drawn to the guitarist, who stood on the far right of the stage, as if he weren't sure he was part of the band.

"He's got a young Robert Downey Jr. thing going on," Karen said, knowing exactly where I was looking. "Except his eyes aren't as buggy."

"He's definitely good-looking," I allowed.

He was lanky and slightly slouched, but in a way that seemed thoughtful rather than lazy. His hair, which needed a trim, was wavy and black.

When it came time for his solo, he turned away from the crowd, too—as if the music were so personal he didn't want a bunch of strangers watching him make it. And because we couldn't see his fingers on the strings, the melody seemed to radiate out from his body in a way that was utterly mesmerizing. Everyone watched him, quiet now, listening to the way the notes soared and plunged through the air.

When it was over we clapped like crazy, and then the band took off their instruments and headed offstage.

And the crazy thing was, when he stepped down from the platform, he walked over to *me*.

My first thought was that he believed I was someone else. So I said, "I'm not—"

"Hi," he said. "Can I buy you a drink?"

Before I could tell him that I had one, Karen slid over to me, grabbed the drink I'd been working on, slipped her spare house key into my pocket, and melted away into the crowd.

I was impressed. And not a little flustered.

"I think your wingman wants you to say yes," the guitarist said, offering me a big, boyish smile. "I'm Rob."

I took his hand and shook it. "Anne," I said. "I'm not from around here, and yes, I'd love a gin and tonic."

But as I followed him toward the bar, I had second thoughts.

Crazy ones.

"Actually?" I said.

He turned around, his dark eyes meeting mine. "What?"

I took a deep breath. "Actually," I said, "I think you should probably just go ahead and kiss me."

Chapter 14

KAREN PLACED a mug of coffee in front of me and then sat down across the breakfast table. "Tell me *everything*," she demanded.

My cheeks grew warm at the memory. (How a person could get to age thirty-six without ever kissing a handsome utter stranger was another mystery, especially considering how fun it had been.) "His name is Rob . . . and we made out a little," I said.

"A little?" Karen asked.

I smiled. Rob and I had gone out to a dark, private corner of the patio, but he hadn't kissed me right away. Instead he'd taken my hand in his and held it, warm and gentle. I traced the calluses on his fingertips from his guitar, and it was almost like I could still hear the melody of their last song. And then I'd blurted, "You know I'm never going to be here again," and he'd smiled this almost bashful smile and said, "Never say—"

But before he could say *never,* I'd stood on my tiptoes and kissed him, a long, deep kiss that sent electric tingles to every single nerve ending in my body. It was the first of several.

"All right, Karen, we made out kind of a lot," I admitted.

"I knew it!" Karen crowed. "I'm so proud of you."

I faked a bow. "Just doing my duty, ma'am. Anytime you need someone to kiss a handsome musician, I'm your gal."

Karen sighed and rested a hand on her still-flat stomach. "I guess I'll have to start living *la vida loca* vicariously through you now."

"I hope you enjoy long hours in the car," I said.

"Did you get his number?"

"No, silly, because I'm leaving, remember?"

She laughed. "You could've called him, said 'thanks for the memories.'"

I shook my head. "That's not *loca,* that's *polite.*" Then out of the corner of my eye, I saw Sophie tiptoeing over in a pair of pink flannel pj's. "Well, look who's up!"

"I made you something," she said shyly, holding out a wrinkled piece of paper.

I squinted at the multicolored lines and squiggles. "I love it — that's an absolutely amazing cat," I said.

"It's actually a guinea pig," she said.

"That's what I meant! Did I say cat? *Obviously* it's a guinea pig." I held it to my chest. "Thank you so much. I have something for you, too." And I pinched off one of the little plantlets that sprouted from Spidey's leaves and placed it in Sophie's tiny palm. "If you put this in potting soil and keep it watered, you'll have your own spider plant."

Her eyes widened. "Does it grow spiders?"

"No, just nice, variegated leaves," I assured her. "Green, with white stripes."

"I want to plant it right now," she said to her mother.

I drained the last of my coffee and stood. "I'll let you two do that. I have to get on the road. I'm going to visit my mom's best friend, near Kansas City."

Karen shot me a look. "That doesn't sound very *loca,* either," she said.

I hugged her and resisted the urge to touch her belly. "I'll see what I can do."

"Don't let another six years go by, okay?" she said.

"I won't," I promised. "I'm coming back to meet those—" I stopped and mouthed the word *babies.*

"Good. And you ought to make one of your own one of these days, you know," Karen said. She always was bossy like that.

"Maybe," I said, though it seemed just as likely that I'd make a spaceship and fly to the rings of Saturn. "Who knows. But I'm going to make a book first." I held up my camera and snapped her picture. "And you're going to be in it."

Chapter 15

I HADN'T seen Pauline, my mom's best friend, for almost two decades. But she sent cards every Christmas, which was how I knew that she'd been diagnosed with breast cancer — just like my mom.

They'd had the same disease, and it had even been caught at the same stage. But only Pauline's story had a happy ending: She'd been cancer-free for five years now.

My mom, on the other hand, had been dead for nearly twenty.

But I didn't want to think dark thoughts on this late-August afternoon, with the sun shining bright and golden over the small town of Bonner Springs, Missouri. So I decided to park on the main drag, buy myself an iced mocha, and walk the quiet streets to Pauline's house while pondering happier subjects.

I passed modest but immaculate houses, roses spilling over white fences, joggers and dog walkers, and even a stand of kids selling lemonade. It was like

strolling along through a Norman Rockwell painting—
which was charming, but also so perfect it was weird.

If I lived in a quaint Midwestern town like this, a palm
tree wouldn't fall on my darkroom—but otherwise,
would my life be so very different? As my dad used to
say, *Wherever you go, there you are.*

But maybe he just used that as an excuse not to go to
new places or, toward the end of his life, to move much
beyond his favorite easy chair. He'd been in a lot of pain
by then—he'd broken a hip, and it hadn't healed right—
so it must have been better to stay still. To wait for death
to find him in the living room.

I shook my head: I was doing a *terrible* job of thinking happier thoughts. So I picked up my pace, hoping
speed would clear my mind a little.

Up ahead, I heard the shrieking whine of a power
saw, and soon after that I smelled the sweet sawdust of
freshly cut wood. As I drew closer, I could see an old
man building something in his garage woodshop.

Normally I would have kept on going, but I was eager
to be distracted. And even from the sidewalk I could
see his confidence in handling the wood, like he'd been
doing it his whole long life. His movements were so
smooth, they almost looked like dance.

When he stopped and lifted his safety glasses to wipe
the sweat from his face, I took a few steps up his driveway.

"Hi there," I called. "I'm sorry for interrupting—but I
just wanted to ask what it is you're making."

He squinted at me for a second, like he was deciding whether to answer. "What I'm making?" he eventually repeated. Then he shook his head and smiled slow and wide. "Well, miss, if you'd really like to know, I am making my own casket."

Chapter 16

*I*took a big step back down the driveway. "Oh dear," I said. "I'm so —"

The old man started to laugh. "It's nothing to be afraid of, young lady," he said. "You can't catch what I've got."

"That's not why —," I began. "I'm not —"

But I was so flummoxed I couldn't finish a sentence.

The old man stopped chuckling and beckoned to me, his face softer now. "Come here," he said. "I might as well show you what it looks like."

I couldn't be rude to a dying person, and so I did what he told me to. I walked into his garage workshop, looked down at the box he was building for his own dead body, and shivered.

You can try to stop thinking about death — but death might not want you to.

He pointed to the nearest corner, where the long side of the casket joined the shorter top end. "See this here? Not a single nail keeping these pieces of oak together. That's what you call a dovetail joint, and it's older than the pharaohs." He ran his hand along the smooth grain and nodded to himself. "I figure what's good enough for Tutankhamen is good enough for me."

"Sure," I said, a little hesitantly. "That seems reasonable."

"Go on," he said. "You can touch it."

I didn't exactly want to. But I did, and the wood felt warm, almost alive, under my fingertips.

Then a door at the back of the garage opened, and a slender white-haired woman poked her head out. "Bob, did you take that casserole out of the deep freeze?" the woman asked. Then she saw me. "Oh, hello there," she said.

"Hi," I said. "I'm just... um, admiring your husband's woodworking."

She gave him a sharp look, then turned back to me. "He's scaring you, isn't he, with his *I might die while you're standing here* talk."

"Actually we hadn't gotten that far," I said. *Thankfully.*

"Bad ticker," Bob said, patting the pocket of his denim work shirt, right over his heart.

His wife pretended to snap a tea towel at him. "Not *that* bad," she assured me. "He got kicked out of hospice last month."

"Wasn't dying fast enough. Not that I complained, mind you," he said.

She smiled at both of us. "My name's Kit. And you are?"

"Anne," I said. "I'm, uh, visiting the Londons up the street."

"Well, Anne, my husband has obviously unnerved you, and I think you need a fortifying cupcake. I made them for my grandson's birthday tomorrow, but I have extras. Hang on." She retreated into the house and came out a moment later with a cupcake for each of us. "I always double the recipe," she said, winking.

"Thank you," I said, feeling grateful but still slightly unsettled.

Bob brushed the sawdust from his hands and took one, too. "Tutankhamen died of gangrene from a fractured leg," he said, between bites. "Gangrene is your body decomposing while you're still alive, you know, and so the pain is unimaginable. He was only nineteen years old."

"Honestly, darling, hush," Kit said. She turned to me. "So you're here to see Pauline London? She's lovely. We're in a book club together."

"She was my mom's best friend," I said. I took a bite of the cupcake, which was rich and chocolaty, with a cream center like a homemade Ho Ho.

Kit's eyes widened. "Was your mother Mary Lynch?"

"Before she was married, yes."

"Oh, I heard all about her! Pauline adored her. She likes to tell how they toured Europe after they graduated—and how they didn't know a thing about the world, and so they stumbled around the continent, innocent as ducklings."

I laughed. "Yeah, I was going to ask her about that. I'm sort of...collecting people's stories."

Kit's face lit up. "I've got one," she said. "Would you like to hear it?"

"Yes, please," I said.

"I know exactly where this is going," Bob mumbled.

"Of course you do. I tell it all the time," she said to him. "It's about Bob and me. How we weren't supposed to meet."

"What do you mean?"

"We'd been set up on a blind date—but not with each other." Kit rested her hand on the coffin as she spoke. "I was supposed to meet my date at this little Italian place. I'd told him I'd be wearing a dress with a flower pinned to it, and that I had black hair. He said he'd be in a blue jacket and a red tie."

"A maroon tie," Bob said. "I had a maroon tie."

"Hush, don't get ahead of me," she scolded.

"So I go to the restaurant, and I see an incredibly handsome young man with a blue jacket and a maroon tie. And I think, *Men are terrible at colors, he probably thinks that's red, poor thing.* And I sit down and we start talking, and we're having a lovely time, and we've just started our entrées when we realize that there's another couple, not two tables away, who look just like us. The woman has black hair and a dress with a flower pinned to it, and the man's wearing *a red tie*." Grinning, she slapped the coffin for emphasis. "I'd sat down across the table from the wrong fellow! Oh, it was so embarrassing. Because by now they'd seen us too! I didn't know what to do. Were we supposed to switch? And Bob says—"

"I said I'd sooner marry her that very minute than

give her up to the guy she was supposed to meet," Bob said.

Kit beamed at him, and Bob reached out and took her hand.

"That's incredible," I said.

"Oh, it's a wonderful story," Kit said. "And it led to a wonderful life."

Bob arced his cupcake wrapper into the trash can. "Tutankhamun was a minor king," he said pensively. "A total nobody back in the dynastic days—but today everyone knows his name. I guess it goes to show you that life is full of surprises." He paused. "Or maybe I should say death is."

Kit shook her head, smiling. "Bob, *really*. Enough with the pharaoh business."

Bob shrugged and then gazed down the driveway out toward the street.

"Would you like another cupcake?" Kit asked.

"No, thank you," I said. "I should get going."

When I looked over at Bob again, I saw that tears were streaming down his cheeks.

"Look at that cardinal," he said. "That same guy's been coming to sit in my Japanese maple for three years now. And I *planted* that tree when we bought the house. My favorite dog's buried over there, by the mailbox. And see where the grass looks lumpy? Our kids dug a big tunnel under the yard one summer, and it's never looked right since. They're all grown up now. Only one lives nearby."

Kit moved to his side and put her arm around him. "Hush, darling," she said.

"The world is so beautiful," he said, softer now. "How am I supposed to leave it?"

It wasn't a question anyone could answer.

Chapter 17

O H MY darling Annie," Pauline said, pulling me in for a hug, "you look just like your mother."

Then she stepped back, wiped her eyes almost angrily, and said, "I'm sorry, dear, I promised myself I wasn't going to cry."

I was feeling a little on the weepy side myself thanks to Bob, so I tried to smile as I said, "That makes two of us."

Watching Pauline as she bustled about in her kitchen, pouring us mugs of mint tea, I tried to imagine what my mom would look like if she were alive. Would she have Pauline's silver hair and crows' feet? Would she be slightly stooped, and just a bit soft around the middle? It was impossible to imagine her as anything but what she'd been — strong and lovely, and then suddenly pale and sick.

"Don't mind the dog," Pauline said, stepping over the prostrate form of an ancient-looking Labrador lying in the middle of the living room carpet. "He's a good old thing but he only wakes up for dinner." She sat down on a brocade couch and patted the cushion next to her. "I got out all my old photo albums for you," she said.

"How did you know?" I asked excitedly.

She smiled. "Daughters always want to see their mothers," she said. "I know you're actually a *professional,* though, so I'm afraid these pictures won't look like much."

But Pauline was wrong—the pictures were perfect. In an album with a fake leather cover, I found a photograph of my mother, smiling at the camera and holding a bouquet of wild violets so big she had to clutch it with both hands. My breath caught in my throat. She was so young—much younger than me—and so beautiful.

"That was in Barcelona," Pauline said, looking over my shoulder. "The night before, we'd gone to see the opera, and Queen Sofía was there, in a box seat. We could see her glittering crown from all the way across the room. But we were so jetlagged—we missed the 'O mio babbino caro' aria, because we both fell sound asleep in our seats."

When I turned the page, I saw my mother and Pauline, their arms around each other, posing in front of a café.

Pauline laughed. "Oh boy. I remember your mother ordered a bean soup there, and it came with something that looked like part of a human finger! We both just about screamed. 'Oh, no, *el cerdo,*' the waiter said. '*La piel!*' It was pork fat, with some skin attached, and apparently she was supposed to eat it. But Annie, it looked like a *knuckle.* So your mother, always polite, took it out of her bowl and hid it in her napkin."

We went through two more albums, with Pauline narrating everything she could remember about their adventures. There was something both beautiful and sad about these pictures from four decades ago. Their colors had faded, and the contrast had lessened, and so everything seemed bathed in a kind of soft golden light.

The color of nostalgia, I thought.

When we'd finished, Pauline turned to me and said, "So that's your mother and me in our youth. What's *your* story, dear?"

"Well actually," I said, "I'm sort of *collecting* stories. Pictures, too. For what I hope will be a book." I pointed to my camera, resting on an end table. "It started when I realized I wasn't really in touch with anyone from my life — not in any real or meaningful way. So I decided to visit people who mattered to me and see what they were up to."

I decided not to add the part about not having a home anymore.

"I'm glad I passed the mattering to you test," Pauline said, smiling. "Your idea sounds like *This Is Your Life,* except that you're in control."

I looked at her blankly.

She laughed. "Oh, you're too young, aren't you?" she said. "It was a TV show where they surprised a person with folks from their past."

"It sounds like reality TV version one point oh."

"It was certainly better than *The Bachelor*," Pauline said dryly. "By the way, that's a fancy camera you've got."

"It's new, and I barely know how to use it," I admitted.

"Have you printed out any pictures?"

"Not yet," I said. "Though my brother gave me a portable wireless printer."

"Well, let's!"

"Do you know how?"

She clucked her tongue at me. "Darling, ten-year-olds are making parkour movies on their iPhones. You and I can work a small printer."

"Speak for yourself," I said, grinning.

I went to retrieve my car and brought in the printer, still in its box. With some trial and error, we managed to set it up, and at Pauline's kitchen table, we printed out all the pictures I'd taken so far. Here was Josh and Kate; there was Ben and my ex.

I shook my head in dismay: the colors weren't right, and I could see pixilation where I should have seen nothing but smooth pigment.

But the compositions were strong, and the power of the faces was undeniable.

"I think you've really got something here," Pauline said.

"Good stories, and the good people who told them," I said, nodding.

Pauline smiled at me. "I'd buy that book," she said.

Chapter 18

*B*UT WHERE would I go to find the next story? That was the question.

Early the following morning, I closed my eyes and pointed my finger at a map of the United States. I'd decided to let fate guide me.

"Denver," I said when I opened my eyes. "That seems as good a place as any, right?"

"And a good bit better than some," Pauline agreed. "I thought you were going to land in the middle of Lake Superior at first, and I doubt you'd get good stories from lake trout."

I traced my finger along the curving blue line of I-70. Denver was probably nine hours west — which meant it was nine hours closer to a place and a person I'd kept in the back of my mind ever since North Carolina.

A destination I couldn't quite admit to myself that I had.

Pauline handed me a paper bag bulging with food for the road and called, "Send me a postcard, dear," as I pulled away.

The weather was gorgeous — the sky bright blue and dotted with pillowy clouds — but the drive grew monotonous quickly. I understood why John Steinbeck took his famous road trip with a standard poodle as opposed to a spider plant.

So when I saw a hitchhiker, standing by the side of the road in the middle of nowhere, it almost seemed like a sign. *Two* hitchhikers, really: a girl and a dog.

I pulled over and rolled down the window. "You need a ride?"

It was an idiotic question — what did I think she needed, a unicorn? But I was nervous, because I'd never picked up a hitchhiker before.

The girl nodded and hurried over, her backpack flapping against her slim hips and her dog bounding after her.

"I assume you're not an ax murderer," I said as she carefully set Spidey on the dashboard and climbed into the passenger seat. Her dog, a pretty yellowish mutt, took its place on the backseat, pressing its nose to the window. "Or a runaway," I added, because I'd just realized just how young she was.

The girl smiled; she had dark eyes, round cheeks with deep dimples, and an unfortunate lip ring. "Thanks for stopping," she said, her voice slightly breathless. "I'm Savannah. That's Lucy."

"And...?" I prodded. As if I was waiting for her to admit that she had an ax in her bag.

"And I used to be a runaway, but then I turned eighteen. So now I'm just an adult without a car. Or a house."

I had to smile then, because now we had something in common. "My name's Anne," I said, "and I don't have a house either."

Savannah nodded like this was totally normal. "I'm so glad you stopped. I was out there for hours," she said. "I had to turn down like six pervy-looking guys. They're happy to give you a ride, but they want something in return, you know?" She gazed out the window over the green fields and sighed. "So where are you going?" she asked.

"Denver," I said. "What about you?"

"Away." She turned around and gave her dog a reassuring pat on the flank. "Just you and me, kid," she said to her.

I watched Savannah out of the corner of my eye. She was vaguely punk looking, with dark short hair and a smattering of freckles across her cheeks. Her clothes were faded and wrinkled, but clean; she'd obviously put major walking miles on her black combat boots.

"Where are you coming from?" I said. "If you don't mind my asking."

She seemed to grimace a little. "Do you want the long story or the short?"

Needless to say, I thought of my book. "The *long*," I said.

She leaned her seat back and said, "Okay, then I have to back up like three years. When, honestly, I was . . . not the greatest kid. But I wasn't the worst, either. I didn't steal or fail all my classes — only geometry, and like, who cares? They're just *shapes*. But I skipped school a lot. My boyfriend's brother was a dealer, and there was always weed and pills around. And I was like, 'Drugs? Sure, I'll take those.' I was fighting all the time with my mom and my stepdad, and I kept telling them that I was going to run away."

"So one day you did," I said.

She shook her head. "No. That's the messed up part." She took a deep breath and then blew it out in a low whistle. "This happened when I was seventeen. I stayed out really late partying one night, and then I went home and passed out in my bed with my clothes and shoes still on. But I woke up super early, and I just knew: *There was someone in my room.* And I sat up and called out, *Who's there?* And the next thing I knew there was a bag over my head, and people were grabbing my arms and legs and pulling me out of my bed. And I was screaming my head off, *Mom, Mom, help! Mommy!!*"

Savannah stopped and turned around to pet Lucy again. I was practically holding my breath.

"I couldn't see anything. I was being *kidnapped*. One person's tying my hands behind my back and the other's half carrying me downstairs. I was still screaming." She paused and shook her head. "And that's when I heard my mom's voice. She said, really quiet, 'Savannah, this is for your own good. You're going to a place where you can be helped.'"

"What?" I gasped.

"These rent-a-cop *thugs* were my 'escorts' to a teen

boot camp," Savannah went on. "You know, like the army for troubled kids? I didn't get to say good-bye to anyone, I didn't get to pack a bag. I just screamed, all the way outside, where they put me in a van and drove me to Idaho. That stunt alone cost my parents five thousand dollars — how sick is that? And I spent the next three months in the woods, chopping logs, digging up stumps, eating slop, and being screamed at. Once I missed curfew and they put me in a cell for two days. Solitary confinement! But then, a few days before I turned eighteen, I ran away."

I was shocked. "What about your parents?" I asked.

"They know I'm safe," she said. "But they can't know where I am."

I shook my head in disbelief. "I'm so sorry," I said.

She shrugged. "We're getting over it, me and Lucy. I mean, I am, and she's helping me. Her people got rid of her, too, didn't they, girl? They sent her to the pound. But I saved her, and now we travel together."

I made the decision right then. "I can take you as far as you need to go," I said. "Wherever that is."

She turned and smiled at me. "Thanks, you're the best. But I think I gotta do this on my own. I'll go with you until—"

"Until Denver," I said firmly. "I'm not letting you out on the side of a highway. And I'm giving you money for a hotel."

"As long as it takes dogs," Savannah said.

"Of course," I said.

"Thank you," she said. "Really. Thanks a lot."

She didn't really want to talk much more after that—it was as if reliving that experience had exhausted her. Or maybe it was just her journey, which was obviously long and complicated.

But I bought her lunch and then dinner, and at seven o'clock that night, I left her in the parking lot of a Best Western on the outskirts of Denver.

She wouldn't let me take a picture of her face, so instead I took a picture of Lucy, sitting by her feet. She wasn't looking at the camera. Instead she was gazing up at the girl she was bound to, and I swear to God she was smiling.

I'd taken a lot of pet pictures in my day, but this, by far, was my favorite.

Chapter 19

An hour later, I checked into a downtown hotel and showered off the eastern Colorado dust. It was still too early to go to bed, and I was too restless to veg out in front of the TV, so I walked down the street until I heard the sound of live music coming from the open windows of a tavern.

I went inside, ordered a gin and tonic, and tapped my foot to the music. When I got my drink, I raised the glass to Savannah and Lucy. I hoped their story would end happily. And I wished I'd ever have a way to know.

"You can join in if you like," someone said.

I turned to see a man about my age, wearing black-framed glasses, with a violin tucked under his arm. He gestured toward the circle of people a few feet away, whose acoustic bluegrass had first pulled me into the bar.

"Now I wandered far away. From my home I've gone astray," sang a woman with a high, clear voice.

I smiled. "Thanks, but I'm not a performer," I said.

"I can tell you play an instrument, though," he said.

I looked at him more carefully. He was handsome

and broad-shouldered, but he squinted like he couldn't see me very well.

"You can? How?" I asked.

"You would've said 'I can't play.' But instead you said you don't perform."

"Very perceptive," I said, smiling. "Okay, I don't play *anymore.*"

"What did you used to play?"

"The violin, actually," I admitted. "In a big high school orchestra, where I could blend in with the crowd. If I screwed up, no one but my stand partner could tell."

He smiled. "We're just here to mess around, and we're a pretty forgiving group," he said. "I'm new to music myself."

I was surprised to hear that. "You seemed really good—for the two minutes I heard you play, anyway."

He sat down on the stool next to me. "I practice four hours a day."

"Wow, I was lucky if I hit twenty minutes," I said.

The bartender placed a beer in front of him and he took a sip before saying, "Doctor's orders."

"The beer?"

He laughed. "No, the practicing."

I could tell there was a story in this, and I leaned forward. "Please tell me how it came to be that a doctor wrote you a prescription for music."

"If you really want to hear it," he said.

"I do."

He told me he'd been a soldier in Afghanistan, riding

in a truck with a soldier from another company, when they hit an IED buried in the road.

"I didn't have my Wileys on," he said, "just a pair of Ray-Bans. So glass and shrapnel went right into my eyes. I couldn't see a thing. I was bleeding all over the other guy, but he managed to clean me up. And then we were stuck there, in the shell of the truck. We were shooting at anything that moved—well, he was; I was shooting blind."

When they weren't shooting, he said, they were telling each other about their lives, because they knew they were more likely to see an RPG heading their way than any kind of rescue vehicle. It seemed like the last conversation they'd ever have with anyone. Eventually, they'd used up their ammunition, and the only thing left to do was take cover and wait.

"I still couldn't really see anything, but he knew the enemy was moving in. And so he covered me with his body—this man I'd never met before in my life. And because of that, he took a bullet to his back."

He stopped for a moment and drank half his beer in what seemed like one long gulp.

"Hard luck poppa standing in the rain," sang the bluegrass folks. "If the world was corn he couldn't buy grain..."

"We made it out alive," he said. "Which was a miracle. But he can't walk, and I can barely see. When I got home, I was so full of anger I didn't know what to do. And then my doctor, who I'd always thought was some

VA quack, told me to learn an instrument. I said, 'I can't see to read music.' And he said, 'That's what your ears are for.' I didn't have the money for a guitar, which is what I really wanted, but my friend had this old violin. So I taught myself how to play it." He patted it where it lay on the bar. "That soldier, Pete, saved my life. But so did this."

"That's an incredible story," I said.

He ducked his head, like *no big deal.* Said, "I've got more where that came from. But let's go play something. You can borrow my violin."

He held it out, insistent, and so I took it from his hands. I tucked the instrument against my neck, feeling the cool smooth bowl of the chin rest. I took the bow in my right hand and curled my fingers around it.

It had been such a long time.

"We'll start with something easy," he said.

And so I played "Barbara Allen," and then "Man of Constant Sorrow," with a group of Colorado strangers, and I wasn't even terrible.

Which is not to say that I was any good, either.

But if that didn't qualify as coming out from behind my camera lens, I didn't know what would.

Chapter 20

THE SUN had barely risen over the Mt. Galbraith foothills when I parked my dirty van in a rutted parking lot and set out along a trail above the city of Golden, Colorado.

I wanted to pause before the next leg of the journey, which was going to be a long one. I wasn't ready to sit behind the wheel for ten straight hours again, for one thing. But there was another reason for the break: it seemed to me that when I arrived at my final destination, my whole *life* could take a turn.

I hiked the rocky path alone for the first hour. My only company was a half dozen hummingbirds that darted through the air on invisible wings. The trail rose through scrubland, with pockets of sage and Ponderosa pine, and I felt wild and alone.

I also felt like I needed to exercise more regularly: after only an hour, I was out of breath and my legs had become Jell-O.

Eventually I crossed paths with a family—two

determined-looking parents and two sullen teenagers, one of whom was staring at his phone while hiking.

I waved and said cheerfully, "Great day for a walk!"

"Whatever," one of the teenagers muttered; the other ignored me completely.

I smiled sympathetically at the mother, thinking, *Good luck with those grouchy children of yours.* But she didn't smile, either, and in fact looked at me quite angrily.

I took a picture of their backs as they walked away. Even their posture seemed affronted. I wanted to call after them, *Hey, if you don't like it, don't do it!*

But it wasn't any of my business, so I kept on walking.

Toward the summit of the mountain I stopped and took in the grand rugged isolation; somewhere out there, in those brown, craggy peaks, was the Continental Divide. I took pictures of the vista, but only because it seemed like I should. It was the pictures of *people* I cared about.

In a way, I felt like I was carrying everyone with me as I traveled. But they weren't baggage; they were more like buoys, lifting me up and nudging me along.

I thought again about what my dad had said— *Wherever you go, there you are*—and I realized that I had to disagree with that. A journey could change a person, and not just by atrophying all her leg muscles.

As I stood above the wild desolation of central Colorado, I could finally admit that I was going to California. And that I was going to call up the first boy I'd ever loved.

And then? I'd just have to see what happened next.

Chapter 21

UTAH PASSED by in an eighty-mile-per-hour blur, and, after a night in a musty Budget Inn, I crossed into Nevada.

The land stretched out flat and dusty on either side of the highway, and on the horizon I could see only barren hills. I'd heard people call Route 50 in Nevada the Loneliest Road in America, but to me, it felt more like the loneliest road on Mars.

After singing every Beatles song I knew, followed by every Bruce Springsteen and then every Rihanna, my throat hurt, my ears rang, and the sound of my own voice was aural torture to me.

This might have been the time I started wishing for something—anything—to break up the monotony. And pretty soon something did.

I heard a *boom,* and right after that the car began to shake and careen to the right. I slammed on the brakes and skidded off onto the gravel shoulder, adrenaline coursing through my veins.

I waited for a few minutes until my panicked heart

slowed. I was fairly certain I knew what had happened, and a look at the right front tire confirmed it: something had punctured the rubber, and it was totally flat.

As I looked in the back for the spare I knew I'd never be able to put on the van, I tried to cheer myself up by thinking about how this would be a good story to tell someday: about how I was stranded for hours on a deserted highway until I got rescued by a long-haul trucker who wasn't at all perverted. Everyone would laugh when I got to the moral: *Be careful what you wish for.*

Then a horn sounded, and a white van pulled up right behind me. An older man with mirrored sunglasses climbed out of the driver's seat and called, "Gas?"

I couldn't believe my luck. I hadn't seen a car for what seemed like two hundred miles, but here was help, just when it was desperately required. "Flat, actually," I said.

He walked over, and as he did, more people got out of the van — eight in total, men and women of varying ages, wearing matching T-shirts that said I WANT TO BELIEVE.

Suddenly I wondered if I was about to be kidnapped by a cult. That would *also* make a great story, assuming I could overcome my indoctrination and somehow escape. I readied myself to run.

"You got Triple A?" the old man asked. He took off his baseball cap, which said THE TRUTH IS OUT THERE, and ran his hands through a shock of white hair.

I shook my head no. You'd think a woman driving

across the country would've signed up for it, but that was just more advice I hadn't taken.

But he didn't bat an eyelash. He just walked around to the back of my van and removed the donut tire. "I think this'll do you until the next service station," he said. "We'll get Jordan to put it on."

A guy who I presumed was Jordan nodded and got to work with the jack and lug wrench.

As we stood there in the windy desolation, I said, "I really, really appreciate this." I tried to think of a polite way to ask if they now expected me to join them, maybe to become one of Jordan's wives. I settled on, "Where are you all headed?"

"South toward Area 51," the old man said. "Did you ever wonder if we weren't alone in the universe? If so — or hell, if not — you're welcome to come along. It's just a little detour."

I hoped my face didn't betray my surprise and delight. These people weren't cultists; they were *UFO hunters* on a *field trip*.

Jordan looked up from my tire. "The last time I went, I saw something shoot across the sky — it must have been going six hundred miles an hour, not too far from me, and it didn't make a sound."

The old man nodded. "Jordan's seen wilder things than most."

I squinted my eyes against the sun's glare and thought about how much this trip had taught me about strangers —

and how, after only a few minutes, they weren't strangers anymore.

Driving south with a vanload of alien-hunters? *That* would be a story.

I glanced at my van, and then over at theirs. Nobody looked insane. I was lonely, and I was supposed to be on an adventure.

I smiled at the old man. I said, "Sure, I'd love to come."

Chapter 22

AFTER JORDAN fixed my flat, I followed them for a few miles to the crossroads, where I pulled my van well off the highway.

"We'll have you back here in ten hours," the old man, who called himself Chili, said. "A lot sooner than any tow truck'd pass by."

And so I became a passenger for the first time in almost two weeks, tucked in the backseat between Marge, who insisted that military scientists were currently reverse-engineering a captured alien spacecraft, and Annie Rose, who claimed to have seen a bright diamond-shaped craft hovering and spinning over an Ohio cornfield last month.

The strange thing was that both of them seemed like intelligent, rational women. Annie Rose, in particular, was well versed in physics; a former professor of applied mathematics, she'd spent her retirement boning up on the possibilities of interstellar travel.

Then the man sitting in front of us, who introduced himself as Mitch, turned around and said, "I bet you haven't heard a story like this. Last summer, I was driving home on a road I'd driven a hundred times before. But when I came around one of the curves, the highway was suddenly completely different. It had eight skinny lanes, and in each lane were dozens of little egg-shaped black cars. The sky was orange, and there were three high, jagged mountains I'd never seen before. And I just knew I'd been teleported to another dimension."

"Personally I think he'd had a few margaritas that night," Marge said, nudging me.

"How'd you get back to this dimension?" I asked.

Mitch shrugged. "I don't know. I just kept driving. And I was praying, you know? Praying so hard I wasn't even breathing. And then the highway turned a corner again, and when I got around that bend, I was back in our world." He paused to let this sink in. "But the thing was, now I was on a totally different interstate than the one I had been on. It took me two extra hours to get home."

"I wish something like that would happen to me," Annie Rose said. "Then I could die happy."

Meanwhile, the landscape we drove through looked more and more extraterrestrial: the flat tops of mesas glowing in the late afternoon sun, the cloudless sky nearly white with heat. *Maybe aliens come here because it looks like their home planet,* I thought wryly.

We reached our destination at dusk and spread out alongside the road. Almost everyone had brought folding chairs, and Chili set up a telescope. As we settled ourselves in, there was hardly a sound, as if everything around us were holding its breath. We watched the stars come out by the thousands. Low above the horizon, Venus shone brightly.

We waited. And waited.

"Please oh please," I heard someone whisper.

Then I saw something streak across the sky, high and fast, and I sucked in my breath.

"What?" Marge said. "Did I miss something?"

"Only a shooting star," Jordan assured her.

"Or, more accurately," Annie Rose said, "the visible path of a meteoroid as it enters the earth's atmosphere."

Jordan snorted, but I felt a twinge of disappointment. Not that I'd really thought I'd see a UFO tonight. And come to think of it, if there *were* evidence of extraterrestrials, I wouldn't want to know about it. Life was complicated enough already—I didn't need an alien species to worry about.

I liked this oddball group of people, though, and part of me wanted them to experience something magical.

But it wasn't to be. After a couple of beautiful but uneventful hours of staring at the stars, Chili said we should probably head back. Oddly enough, no one seemed that disappointed.

"It's like fishing," Mitch told me. "You can't always catch a prizewinning bass."

"But the fish can't laugh at you," Marge pointed out. "That's what the aliens are doing. Looking down on us

from superconductor-powered spaceships and hootin'
and hollerin' over how *dumb* we are."

"Speak for yourself," Mitch said, laughing, and Marge
swatted him on his elbow.

I wanted to keep listening to their stories, but it was
after midnight and the humming of the wheels on the
asphalt quickly lulled me to a dreamless sleep. I didn't
wake until they'd pulled up to my van.

It was still predawn when, bleary-eyed, I thanked my
new friends and climbed into the driver's seat.

And then I drove west, as the sun rose in a fiery blaze
behind me.

Chapter 23

ᴮᴇᴄᴀᴜsᴇ ɪ stopped in Carson City to get a new tire, I didn't arrive in Sonoma, California, until late afternoon. From a coffee shop on the square, I booked a last-minute Airbnb. I'd reached the end of the road, after all—and last night I'd slept in the alien-hunters' van—and so I figured I could justify the splurge.

The cottage was cedar-shingled, surrounded by a wild, flowering garden and perched above a small vineyard. To the west lay green rolling hills dotted with enormous oak trees. The owners of the cottage, who lived in a big house a hundred yards away, had kindly left me a bottle of wine and a platter of fruit, cheese, and bread.

After devouring every last crumb on the plate, I took a walk along the one-lane road as night fell. The air smelled like late roses and eucalyptus, and I could hear the croak of frogs and the chirp of crickets. I walked slowly, aimlessly. There was no reason to hurry because I was no longer going anywhere. I'd arrived.

All I had to do now was send an email.

But instead, after my walk, I sat at a small writing desk and scratched out the postcards I'd bought at various gas stations—to Bill, to my brother, to Lorelei and Sam and Karen and Pauline—so they'd know I was still alive.

And only then did I get out my computer and begin the email I'd driven three thousand miles to write.

Dear Julian,
Long time no see!

No, too chipper—too neighborly.

Dear Julian,
This is going to come way out of left field, but I

That wasn't going to work either.

Hey Julian!
It's the ghost of your girlfriend past.

As if.

Dear Julian,
It's been almost 19 years since I last saw you, sitting in the passenger seat of a U-Haul pointed toward Cambridge.

This really wasn't going very well.

I opened the bottle of wine, poured myself a glass, and took a fortifying sip. If I could survive a hurricane, leave my life behind, and set off across the country in the hopes of writing a book, I could certainly write an email to an old flame.

Dear Julian,
I happen to be in town for a day or two, and I was wondering if you'd like to have lunch. It's been a long time, and it'd be great to catch up.

Anne

I took a deep breath, held it, and hit Send.

Immediately thereafter, I got up and began pacing the room.

I'd met Julian on the side of a road—just like the alien-hunters. I'd been walking home from school when the gray June sky unleashed a torrential, biblical downpour. I was soaked in seconds, sloshing my way through sudden puddles, when Julian pulled up on a motorcycle and offered me a ride. He went to the boarding school on the other side of town, but I'd seen him at a few parties. I glanced at his little vintage Honda, which hardly looked big enough for him, and I shook my head.

He'd smiled. "A gentleman always sees a lady to her door," he said—or that's what I thought he said; it was impossible to hear in all that pounding rain. He took off his helmet and put it on my head, and then he patted my hand reassuringly. And because his hand was so gentle, and because I was sopping and I still had a mile to go, I climbed on the back of the bike and put my arms around his waist.

It was the scariest ride of my life. The rain lashed my body and the gusting wind seemed like it was going to blow us into a ditch. Because I was squeezing my eyes shut in terror, I didn't notice that he'd made a wrong turn until we were two miles into the country.

"*Stop,*" I'd screamed, and he'd yelled "*What?*" And then I nearly made him lose his balance and crash as I gestured wildly to a farm up ahead.

Shivering, we waited out the rest of the storm in a barn, watched by two wary cows and a few twittering sparrows.

Maybe it was the near-death experience (or the *near*-near-death experience) that made us feel close to each other so quickly. Or maybe it was the serendipity of two bookish introverts finding each other in such a crazy way. Or it could have been something as simple as teenage hormones. But after that day, we were together all the time—we talked on the phone every night before we fell asleep, and we saw each other every weekend. He gave me flowers and mix CDs; I bought him poetry books, a collection of Rilke's letters, and weird talismans from thrift shops.

When Julian went away to college, I thought my heart would break. But later that fall my mother died, and the pain of that washed away everything else.

It wasn't that I thought I'd fall in love with Julian again all these years later. But I needed to see who he'd become.

And, to be quite honest, his Facebook status was *single*.

My email dinged, and my heart did a jitterbug in my chest.

I'd love to meet, his reply said.

Let's say the El Dorado Kitchen at the El Dorado Hotel. Tomorrow at noon.

Yours,
Julian

Chapter 24

I was early to the restaurant, even though I'd spent two hours getting ready, including thirty minutes of debate over whether I should wear my hair up (sophisticated) or down (carefree).

Ultimately I'd decided on an elegant chignon, complemented by my best sundress, my biggest pair of dark sunglasses, and my only pair of heels. No one would mistake me for a modern-day Audrey Hepburn, but I felt put together—chic, even.

The maître d' smiled graciously and led me to the restaurant's back patio. There, sitting in the dappled shade of a lush fig tree, was Julian.

My breath caught in my throat; the years since I'd seen him evaporated in an instant. Here he was, the boy I thought I'd love forever, suddenly transformed into a man.

As I walked toward him, my whole body electric with recognition, Julian looked up from the book he was reading, and his face opened in that big smile I knew so well. He stood up, and we hugged—laughing, shy, elated. He kissed me softly on the cheek and then stepped back to take me in.

"You're even more beautiful than I remembered," he said as he pulled out a chair for me.

"You're not half bad yourself," I countered, blushing and pushing a loose strand of hair away from my face.

But that was an understatement: Julian was striking, with high, aristocratic cheekbones and a light fan of wrinkles around his bright green eyes. His hair was a shade darker than it used to be, and he'd traded the vintage T-shirts and faded jeans of his youth for summer-weight wool pants and a custom shirt.

He looked so handsome and prosperous — if I hadn't known him as a skinny teenager, I'd probably be too intimidated to talk to him now.

As I settled myself at the table, a waiter glided over and poured me a flute of Champagne. "Will you be having the four-course tasting menu also?" he murmured. "The ahi tuna salad, the tagliatelle with fresh herbs, the king salmon, and the zabaglione?"

The what? I thought. My mind was spinning a little. For one thing, my first love was sitting three feet away from me. For another, my road meals were basically four courses of Cheetos. I must have nodded, though, because the waiter said "Very good" and slid away.

"Nearly twenty years," Julian said, shaking his head and smiling. "I can't believe it."

"I know," I said, taking a sip of the golden bubbly wine. "It's crazy, isn't it? I'm almost twice as old as I was the last time I saw you. So why is it, Julian Fielding, that I so rarely feel like a real grown-up?" I laughed. "Do you ever have that problem? You don't really look like you do."

Julian's eyes sparked with humor. "I'm a true grown-up from approximately nine to five, Monday to Friday. Your typical working stiff. Other than that, all bets are off."

"What do you do now, anyway?" I asked. My haphazard Facebook sleuthing had turned up little besides his relationship status—Julian wasn't much of a poster.

"I'm a lawyer," he said. "And I'm glad you couldn't immediately guess that. I specialize in estates and trusts. But that's all you need to hear about my job, because it's deadly boring."

"Oh, but very respectable," I said, a slight lilting tease in my voice.

"Yes, that's what I always meant to be when I grew up: respectable," Julian said wryly.

"Well, I wanted to be an art photographer, and instead I take pictures of pets. Weddings. Bridezillas. I guess that's just what happens when you get older: You have to get realistic. You compromise." I sighed as I speared a lettuce leaf.

Julian smiled. "But if being a grown-up means you can leave work to take a long lunch with a gorgeous woman, then I'll take it."

I flushed again, wondering how in the world he was still single.

"So what brings you to town, anyway?" Julian asked.

You, I wanted to say.

What I actually said was "I'm working on a new project — it's a mix of words and pictures at the moment. I've been informally interviewing people all over the country about their lives, their stories. And I've been taking their photographs."

"That sounds amazing," Julian said.

"I don't know about amazing, but I hope it's at least *interesting*," I said.

Julian pointed his fork at me in mock exasperation. "Still self-deprecating after all these years. When are you going to accept the fact that you're brilliant and talented and that whatever you do is going to work out?"

"Well, my marriage sure didn't work out," I said dryly. Then I felt like an idiot, because I hadn't meant to bring that up at all.

But Julian smiled with both sympathy and understanding. "Marriage is undoubtedly complicated." He seemed about to say something, but then he took a sip of wine.

"Were you married too?" I asked.

Julian gazed down at the plate of herbed pasta that had just been placed between us. "Actually I still am," he said.

Chapter 25

*W*HAT?"

Because Julian was winding a piece of tagliatelle around his fork, he didn't see my shock.

"But probably not for much longer," he added, looking up.

"I had no id—I'm so sorry," I said.

I couldn't believe how close we'd once been, and how little we knew of each other now. "Can I ask..." But then I stopped.

"I used to tell you everything, didn't I?" Julian said. He gave a little one-shouldered shrug. "I see no reason to stop now. Sarah, my wife, was a ballet dancer. As you can probably imagine, it's a beautiful but brutal business. She'd struggled for years with an eating disorder, but by the time we met she was healthy. We married five years ago on Mykonos, and not long after that she decided that she wanted to have a baby."

"And you?" I asked.

He smiled. "I can't pretend I was excited by the thought of wiping some squalling infant's bottom, but I came around," he said. "We tried for a long time, and after almost two years, she got pregnant. We were elated. But then she miscarried. When she got pregnant again, she miscarried again. And again."

"You're kidding," I breathed, knowing that he wasn't. "I'm so sorry."

I'd been expecting a story of infidelity like mine, but this was a pain I couldn't even imagine.

"She had five miscarriages in two years. The last one was at sixteen weeks; he had tiny little fingernails. He seemed...so perfect." Julian took a glug of wine. "It just took too big of a toll on her—I think because she felt like somehow it was her fault. That she'd made her body incapable of carrying a child. She left town three months ago. I think she's on a silent retreat in Sedona, but I honestly don't know. And I don't know if she's coming back."

I was at a loss for words. "That sounds so *hard*."

"I won't lie and say it isn't." He was quiet for a little while, and then he leaned forward and patted my hand. "But for you, my long-lost Annie, this is supposed to be a celebratory lunch. Let's not talk about what's gone wrong. Let's think about what's lucky instead. Like me logging into my old email account last night, which I almost never check, and seeing a message from you."

That *was* luck. What would I have done if Julian hadn't written back? Wandered around the plaza for hours or even days, hoping to run into him? I'd tried something like that once before.

"You're doing a terrible job on your wine, by the way," Julian added.

I knocked the whole glass back; I felt like I needed it. "Better?"

He laughed. "A little déclassé, maybe, but definitely more efficient."

He refilled my flute to the very rim, and by the time dessert appeared, I was feeling slightly tipsy.

"Maybe we should go take a nap in the plaza," I said, almost meaning it.

Julian raised an eyebrow at me. I assumed I was being déclassé again, until he borrowed a blanket from the hotel's concierge on our way out of the restaurant.

In the wide green plaza, the sun was hot and the breeze deliciously cool. Near the duck pond, in the shade of a huge oak, Julian spread out the blanket.

We lay down, lightheaded with Champagne. I watched the leaves dance across the sky above us and talked about some of the things I wanted to see while I was there.

"I can't believe you're here," Julian said, interrupting. "The girl who got away."

I turned to look at his strong profile. "That's how you thought of me? That's how I thought of *you*. You went away. I stayed."

Julian was staring up at the clouds. "I used to think about you a lot. For years. I wondered what you were doing and where you were. I wanted to know if you were happy, and if you'd moved to New York like you'd said you were going to, and if you'd ever gotten back on a motorcycle."

"I thought about you, too," I said. "I wondered if you'd kept playing the guitar. And if you still wrote poetry. Or if you'd gotten too serious and respectable." I nudged him lightly to let him know I was teasing.

He smiled. "No, I don't write poetry. I should dust off my old guitar, though." He paused. "It's good to start things back up again sometimes," he said quietly.

I decided not to think too hard on what he might mean by that. We were lying close to each other on a linen blanket on an August afternoon, full with good food and good wine. I could let that be enough for now.

Then Julian's phone rang, and he looked at it and sighed. "I'm sorry, Anne, I have to run—I'm late for a meeting."

Reluctantly we got up, and then we kissed, ever so quickly, on the lips.

"Lunch was wonderful," he said. "I'll call you tomorrow."

"Good-bye," I called.

He stopped and turned around in a halo of sunlight. *"Hello,"* he said, grinning. And then he hurried away.

Chapter 26

THE PHONE woke me as the sun was just rising over the vineyard. I knew it was Pauline on the other end of the line, but for a few seconds all I heard was sobbing. "Bob Kline died last night," she finally said.

I gasped, even though part of me had known what she was going to say. "But Kit said—"

"Everyone thought he had another year at least. But Annie, no one knows anything in the end, do they? The funeral's at Grace Episcopal on Friday. Oh, poor, poor Kit."

"Poor Bob," I whispered.

I wondered if his kids had come home for the weekend for the birthday party—if he'd been able to see them once more before he died. And I wondered, too, if he'd finished his coffin, and could now be buried in it.

When Pauline and I hung up, I paced around the cottage. Maybe it was strange to mourn someone I'd met only once, but I couldn't deny my sadness.

When anxious, uneasy and bad thoughts come, I go to the sea, Rilke had written in a letter to his wife, a line I've never forgotten. I'd been thinking about driving to

Point Reyes National Seashore, and now, because of Bob, I would do it.

Maybe it would bring me comfort.

I could smell the ocean even before I saw it glimmering blue-gray in the distance. The briny air was so familiar that for a confusing split-second, I thought I was returning home instead of driving ever farther away from it.

My skin began to tingle, already anticipating the chilly shock of water.

Except for a woman and her dog in the distance, there was no one else on the beach. I took off my shoes and dug my toes into the cool sand.

The tide was coming in, and each wave slid closer to me than the last. Eventually, the water flowed over my feet and swirled around my ankles. I gritted my teeth and nearly yelped: it was so much *colder* than the Atlantic.

Rilke wrote that we should love life so much that we'd love death, too; death, after all, was just life's other half. But I didn't think I could ever love that kind of destruction. I doubted that Bob could, either—or my parents, for that matter, or anyone else who had to leave life's party before they were ready.

When the breeze picked up and whipped my hair into my face, I remembered the gusty morning of Hurricane Claire. Strangely, it felt like a lifetime ago. As I stood there, rooted in the sand, my feet grew numb with cold, and eventually I began to cry. I told myself this was a good place to do it: once my warm, salty tears fell into the cold, salty ocean, no one would be able to tell them apart.

Then through bleary eyes I saw someone coming toward me on the sand—a tall figure, walking quickly and waving.

I squinted in the bright sunshine.

It was Julian.

Chapter 27

*H*E WAS wearing a dark suit and Italian loafers; he looked handsome and utterly out of place on the wind-swept beach.

"Julian?" I asked, incredulous—as if it could possibly be someone else.

"You'd said you might come out here today," he explained. "And when you didn't answer my texts...." His voice trailed off.

I sniffled and tried to wipe my eyes discreetly. I hoped it wasn't obvious that I'd been crying. "But why are you here?"

"I haven't stopped thinking about you since yesterday," he said.

I didn't know what to say to that. "But what—"

"Say you'll spend the afternoon with me," he interrupted.

I turned toward the water again. As the wave receded it seemed as if the ocean were pulling away from me. Why on earth would I say no? "All right," I said. "Of course."

"Can we walk?" he asked.

He was gazing at my bare feet; he seemed to have a hard time meeting my eyes. Yesterday he'd been so cool and charming, but today he seemed skittish. Nervous.

We walked along the beach in silence for a little while. Then, because someone had to say *something,* I asked, "How was your meeting yesterday?"

Julian sighed. "Well, that particular client wants to leave his body to science and his money to his pet llama, if you can believe it," he said. "When I suggested that there were more deserving beneficiaries—for the money, anyway; science can have the old codger if it wants him—he *smirked* at me. I *loathe* smirking and anyone who does it. I can't even stand the word itself." He shook his head. "Wait, why am I going on like this?

"I asked," I said, following him as he veered off the beach and onto a narrow path that wound between high, grassy dunes.

"I think he's just pulling my leg, honestly, and he's got so much money that it doesn't matter if he's paying me three hundred an hour to do it."

"Maybe he's lonely," I suggested.

"Then he could play golf, or join the Elks. I have better ways to spend my time." Julian swiped at a clump of beach grass, and then he smiled to himself. "Like taking a walk with Anne McWilliams, formerly of Andover, Massachusetts."

"Thank you, I'm flattered," I said, laughing. "Even if a grouchy old weirdo doesn't offer much in the way of competition."

We turned a corner, and the path narrowed even more before stopping at the far end of the dunes. But we weren't at the parking lot now, which I'd expected. Instead, we were standing at the edge of a manicured green lawn, dotted with clusters of Adirondack chairs. A hundred yards away stood a small, quaint seaside inn.

Our conversation, which had barely begun, stopped immediately. I suddenly understood why Julian had come to find me.

He finally looked me in the eyes, and I looked back at him. I knew what he'd hoped would happen next.

And almost imperceptibly, I nodded.

Chapter 28

WE WALKED into the lobby, where Julian paid for a room. We didn't say anything until we were standing in the middle of a suite with yellow wallpaper and French doors that opened onto a tiny patio. My cheeks felt hot—whether from sun or self-consciousness, I wasn't sure.

"The obligatory bottle of Napa Chardonnay," Julian said, lifting a bottle from its bucket of ice. "A glass?"

I took it with slightly trembling hands and set it down without taking a sip. I noticed he did the same.

Then we smiled at each other, not quite certain how to begin.

"May I kiss you?" Julian asked softly.

It was so romantic—so silly—that he asked. That was why we were *here*. But he'd always been a gentleman, even at seventeen.

I nodded and moved toward him. Taking a deep breath, I slid my hands around his waist and tilted my face up toward his. He hesitated for a single instant, and then he leaned down. His kiss was so tender that I thought I might cry again.

It had been such a long time.

Our mouths quickly grew hungry. I took his bottom lip between my teeth because he used to like it when I did that. He slipped off my shirt and then my bra. His hands, his devouring kisses, were everywhere. I felt like every nerve was singing.

"Let me look at you," he whispered.

I lay down on the bed and let him take me in. I knew that I'd changed, that I wasn't the radiant, blossoming thing I'd been the last time we saw each other, but I didn't care; right here, right now, I loved my body more than I ever did when I was young. Julian wasn't the skinny poet boy he'd been, either; his chest was broad and tanned and no longer hairless. I reached out and pulled him to me, skin to skin.

"This is a little crazy," he whispered into my neck. "I don't know what this means."

"I don't know either," I said. "But that doesn't matter."

Then I kissed him again, harder, more insistent. We didn't have to know what we wanted from each other, because our *bodies* knew. They remembered everything.

Afterward, lying next to me, Julian said, "I think you should stick around for a while."

"Like until your wife gets back to town?" I asked. I was trying to be lighthearted, but it came out wrong.

He sucked in his breath.

"I'm sorry," I said. "I didn't mean that the way it sounded."

He ran his hands through his tousled hair. "It's not unfair, Anne. I'm *not* divorced; I haven't filed any papers. I've just been waiting. But not for Sarah to come back to me. It's more like I've been waiting for some kind of sign, some reason to act. And maybe that's you."

I pulled the sheet up to my chin. "I don't want to be the reason for anyone's divorce."

"Not the reason," Julian said. "The...encouragement."

I took a deep breath. "You know, there's something I never told you," I said. "After my mom died, I went to Cambridge. With Karen. We skipped school one day and drove there."

"To see me?" Julian asked.

I nodded. I hadn't thought of this trip in years, but now the memory had come rushing back. "I couldn't call you back then. I couldn't write you. But I wanted to *see* you. So the two of us wandered around Harvard Yard for hours. It was spring, and the lilacs were blooming, and everything was lush and beautiful. We were so excited at first! Then we got bored because you didn't appear, and then, another hour or two later, we decided that we were completely crazy. Harvard has thousands of students—why in the world did we ever think we'd see you?"

"I can't believe you didn't tell me you were coming," Julian said.

"But the crazy thing was, we *did* see you. We were

getting ready to leave and suddenly there you were, in front of the library, with your backpack over your arm and your ratty Bob Dylan T-shirt under your Ralph Lauren button-down. You looked so at home, and so happy, in a place I could never get into—or pay for if I did. I think that's when I realized that you and I weren't meant to be. That we didn't belong together."

Julian frowned ever so slightly. "I don't understand," he said.

I tried to explain. "Take me and Karen," I said. "We were so unlike each other that I used to think we were basically two different species," I said. "But animals of two different species can be friends. Like a gazelle and a tortoise, for example—no problem. There are entire books about cross-species buddies. But animals of two different species can't *mate*."

Julian reached for my hand. "Anne, I hate to say it, but you're still not making sense."

"I'm sorry," I said. "It's confusing to me, too, and probably the animal metaphors aren't helping. But I think the point is that for a little while, our two different worlds overlapped. And when they did, we had something wonderful. And this, *right now,* is wonderful. But it isn't real, Julian. This is memory. This is us paying a visit to our old selves before we figure out who our new ones are."

"I don't know that I agree with you," he said quietly.

I leaned over and kissed him on the cheek. "That's okay. You don't have to," I said.

He took a long, slow breath. "So what are we going to do now?" he asked.

"Let's take that nap we didn't take yesterday," I said. I turned toward him and put my arm across his warm stomach. "I could use the sleep. I have a really long drive ahead of me."

Chapter 29

FUELED BY coffee, doughnuts, and a giant bag of chocolate-covered espresso beans, I made the twenty-six-hour drive to Bonner Springs in two days. It had been hard to say good-bye to Julian, but I knew it was the right thing to do. He belonged to my past, and my future—whatever it was—lay somewhere else.

I could certainly wait to start worrying about it until after Bob Kline's funeral.

Pauline and I drove to the church together. She sat stony-faced in the passenger seat. "I did all my crying last night," she said. But I could see tears glittering in the corner of her eye.

The small church was nearly overflowing with people. Sunlight streamed through stained-glass windows, and fragrant lilies spilled out of tall vases in the sanctuary. Everything looked so beautiful, it almost seemed like a celebration—except for the fact that there, front and center, was the coffin I'd watched Bob make, white rose petals scattered across the lid.

When it came time for the eulogy, Kit Adams couldn't

speak; she shook her head mutely, tears streaming down her face, until a man rose and carefully helped her down from the pulpit. Then he took her place and stood there silently for a moment, looking out at all of us, a faint, sad smile on his lips.

He was tall, with dark hair that had obviously been cut for the occasion. He wore a dark suit but no tie. He was tan, like someone who worked outside, and he gripped the sides of the pulpit with strong, calloused hands. I felt a flicker of recognition when his eyes met mine, because I saw again Bob's intense, dark-eyed gaze.

The man took a deep breath and cleared his throat. "My father was a lucky man," he began. "Although it didn't start out that way. His childhood wasn't easy: He was the kid with the too-big shoes, newspaper stuffed in the toes, and the pants that were more patches than pants. The kid who ate government cheese and who didn't have a dad. The kid whose mom worked so hard, trying to provide for him, that she was hardly ever home. But she loved him and encouraged him, and he worked as hard as she did. He went to school and he studied like crazy and—" The man stopped and shook his head. "Oh, boy, this sounds pretty boilerplate, doesn't it? Another story of pulling yourself up by your boot-straps. The cliché of the American Dream. Well, I'm sorry, but it's true. My dad believed in luck, without a doubt, but only if you worked hard enough to deserve it—which he did. One day when he was twenty-two, he had the luck of walking into the *Kansas City Star* about five minutes after the old crime beat reporter had quit in a huff. That's how he became a journalist." He looked up and almost smiled. "Although my dad would have me remind you that he was also a very good carpenter, especially once he retired.

"Anyway, not long after he became a reporter, he had the luck to get his Friday night plans mixed up, and he met my mother on a date she was supposed to be on with someone else. After they married, he went to Vegas for a conference, where he played craps for the first time ever. He walked away with enough money to buy a BMW—a used one, but *still*. When I was six, I wanted to play baseball, so he got a glove and started playing in the backyard, and pretty soon he joined a club team for kicks. He got so good that a scout from the Royals farm team came out to take a look at him." He paused, and this time he smiled for real. "They didn't want him, because he was too old, but that's beside the point." Laughter now mixed with the sound of sniffles.

"And he was beyond lucky to know and love all of you," the man went on. "Even having a bad heart was lucky. My father didn't want to die, any more than you or I do, but when death came for him, it was quick and merciful. I believe in luck and magic because he did. I am a lucky man because Robert James Kline was my father."

Bob Kline's son stopped, turned toward the coffin, and held his hands over his heart. And then he stepped down from the pulpit and sank into a pew.

I cried hard then—for Bob and his family most, but also for everyone in that church. Because we'd all lost a lot over the course of our lives, and we would lose still more. Not even luck would save us from that.

But the tears were cleansing, and I welcomed them.

Chapter 30

WHEN THE service was over, everyone moved to the church courtyard, where a buffet lunch had been set up under a large white tent. I wasn't hungry, but I could appreciate the spread of fried chicken, ribs, baked beans, and potato salad—the kind of old-fashioned, stick-to-your-ribs dishes I hadn't had in years.

Pauline walked over to me, followed by Bob's son, who, unlike the rest of us, had made it through his eulogy without crying. But he looked paler now. Exhausted.

"This is Anne," she said to him curtly, as if neither he nor I needed any other explanation for the introduction. And then she walked away, wiping her eyes and sniffling. A moment later, she turned back around and called, "You know what to do."

I looked at Bob's handsome son and thought, *I hope she's talking to him, because I sure don't.*

The son offered me a slightly discomfited smile. He was probably a year or two younger than me, and at least eight inches taller.

"Hello, Anne," he said as we shook hands. "I'm Jason. Jason Kline. Though I guess that last part's obvious."

"I'm so sorry for your loss," I said. I knew he'd heard it a thousand times today, but what else could I offer?

"Thank you," he said. He sounded genuinely grateful. Then he added, "My dad told me about you."

"He did?" I asked. I shifted nervously from one foot to the other. "Did he say, 'So there was this crazy lady who walked up and asked me about the coffin'?"

"It's technically a casket, actually. A casket has four sides, but a coffin has six, plus the top and the bottom. Think of what Dracula slept in—that's a coffin." Then he stopped. "Sorry, does that seem condescending? Or maybe just morbid, even for a funeral?"

"I don't know. I'm feeling confused in general," I admitted. "Like why I'm so sad, and why I'm even here. I mean, your father was a wonderful man, that was obvious to me. But I met him for all of an hour. And here I am, thousands of miles from where I live, mourning him in a dress that isn't even black because I've been traveling and I don't have one."

Jason's smile grew warmer. "He told me you were 'a good one.' He said I ought to tell you that if I ever met you. I know he'd be glad you were here."

"That's so kind, though I barely understand why."

"He just liked you right off," Jason said. "He fancied himself an excellent judge of character."

"As well as an excellent carpenter," I said.

"Exactly," Jason said. "I also think you gave him a chance to appreciate his life. Not that he hadn't before, of course. But looking back on it with you—a perfect stranger—he saw it all over again for the wonderful thing it was."

"So maybe the moral of the story is 'be kind to strangers,'" I said. "I feel like that's something I've been learning lately."

"Be grateful for what you have, and be nice to people," Jason agreed. "I think most people are pretty decent at heart, don't you?"

I nodded in agreement. Everyone I'd met on this trip had been damn near great.

Jason looked down at the ground for a moment before looking up and meeting my eye again. "My dad said something else. But it's going to sound crazy."

I said, "I don't mind crazy."

"He said that I was supposed to ask you out for dinner."

"Really?" I asked, taken aback.

"Really. He said, *Son, take my advice for once.*"

I had to laugh then. "You have trouble with that, too?"

"Very much," he said.

"So in that case you're *not* asking . . . ," I began.

"Yes I am," he said. "I'm asking you out to dinner. At my dad's funeral. I know it's nuts. I know you live a thousand miles away. And I know I'm going to start crying halfway through the first course. But I'm doing what he told me to do, because I don't know if I'll ever see you again. And I *know* I won't see him ever again. So, will you go? There's a nice little Italian place..."

I paused. I thought about all I'd done and seen on my journey so far, and how every single day, I'd had to be open to chance.

To sorrow, too.

And to luck.

"Yes," I said. "I'd love to go to dinner with you."

Jason reached out and slipped the camera strap off my shoulder.

"Smile," he said.

"But—"

"For my dad?"

"I can't," I said. "I hate having my—"

"What did King Tut say when he fell down and hurt himself?" Jason interrupted. *"I want my mummy!"*

And I laughed—because it was so stupid and because from now on I'd never hear anything about Tutankhamen without remembering Bob Kline. While I was laughing, Jason snapped the picture.

"Perfect," he said. "Now you can have your story in the book, too." Seeing my look of surprise, he explained. "Pauline told me all about it when I was here last weekend. Your project sounds amazing."

"Thank you," I said, taking the camera back from him. "I can't tell my best story, though."

"Why not?"

I shrugged. "I guess because I'm still in the middle of writing it," I said.

Jason smiled. "Death notwithstanding, I hope this is a good chapter," he said.

I smiled back at him. "I like the direction it's going in," I said.

Chapter 31

A YEAR ago, I never could have imagined the turns my life would take. It was possible that having foresight—like taking advice—was one of my weak points.

But it was a flaw I could live with.

"Anne!" A small, red-haired woman in towering black stilettos interrupted my thoughts. "I'd like you to meet Sasha Delaney. She's an art critic for *LA Weekly*."

I smiled at Amy, my new gallerist, and then I shook the hand of a statuesque young woman. "Thank you so much for coming," I said.

"Your show's wonderful," Sasha said. "I'd love to talk to you about your process. Although maybe it'd be easier when you're not swamped by opening-night guests." She handed me her card.

"I'd love to," I said calmly, even though my brain was short-circuiting with excitement.

"Call me Monday," Sasha said. "It was so good to meet you. Now I'm going to see if I can get a glass of wine before the throngs drink it all."

I gazed around the crowded gallery with a mix of happiness and disbelief. Printed on archival paper and suspended in beechwood frames, my poster-size photographs looked almost monumental on the clean white walls. Next to them, hung casually with thumbtacks, were the much smaller prints I'd made with my portable printer. But to me, the most exciting part of my show was in the center of the gallery, where a long handmade table, polished to a perfect sheen, held stacks of my new book, *A Thousand Words*.

In it were pictures of all the people I'd met, with their stories handwritten below their portraits. Here was Pauline on page four, clutching her beloved photo albums; opposite her was the mechanic, leaning against my beloved Beatrice. There was Lucy the dog, gazing up at her girl; next to her, Kate the waitress posed with her Melitta coffeepot, her smile radiant and proud.

I'd taken a lot of new pictures for the book, too. My neighbor Bill leaned against a shovel in front of my house as he took a break from overseeing its reconstruction. "I was born in the Kentucky hills on the night of a blood moon," his story began, "in a year so long ago I'm damn near ashamed to admit it."

A few pages further on was a photograph of my brother, eating breakfast a few months ago at Barnacle Bill's; his story about sneaking out one night and witnessing an attempted robbery was definitely one my parents never heard.

Thanks to all the pictures, I felt surrounded by my

friends and family, even though I barely knew anyone in the room.

I'd met Amy, the red-haired owner of this up-and-coming Los Angeles gallery, by pure chance. I was on my way back to North Carolina, and she was visiting her aging mother. Seated at neighboring café tables, we'd struck up a conversation. She'd asked me what I did, I told her about my project, and one thing, as they say, led to another.

It was so surprising, so serendipitous, that it felt like winning the lottery. But that comparison didn't really do it justice, because a lottery was only about money. This show, on the other hand, was about having a very old dream—a dream so old I'd almost forgotten it—finally, finally come true.

"It's pretty incredible, isn't it?"

I turned to find Jason Kline at my side, a plastic cup of complimentary sparkling wine in each hand. I smiled as I took one from him.

"Yes, that table you made really steals the show," I said.

He grinned. "That wasn't what I was talking about," he said.

"I know." I stood up on my tiptoes and kissed him on the cheek, and he put his arm around my shoulders. "Thank you for coming," I said.

He shrugged. "It was only a seven-hour drive. With a U-Haul. And a really big table bouncing around in it."

"You have only yourself to blame," I pointed out.

As I'd learned on the night of our epic, amazing,

eight-course dinner, Jason built custom furniture out of a workshop in Tucson, Arizona. And so, a month later, when I'd called to tell him about my show, he'd had the brilliant idea to make me a table.

I guess we were both looking for excuses to see each other again — and furniture seemed as good as any.

I didn't really know what was going on between us, and probably he didn't either. Right now, our lives were two thousand miles away from each other. But, as I knew better than most, life could change in an instant.

"I'd kind of like to buy the portrait of the dog," Jason said. "Do you offer a friends and family discount?"

I shrugged. The gallery had priced the pictures so high, I couldn't even afford my own work. "Who knows?" I said, laughing. "I'm not the boss around here — that's Amy."

Jason squeezed me a little tighter. "Well, do you think your boss might let you clock out a little early tonight?"

I looked around at the crowd of well-heeled strangers nodding approvingly at my work. Amy's assistant had already put little red dots next to many of the portrait titles, which meant my show was actually *selling*. And the stacks of books? They were getting smaller every minute.

All in all, things were going about as well as they possibly could, which was better than I'd ever dared to imagine.

"I *am* really hungry," I said. "Do you know a nice Italian place around here?"

Jason said, "As a matter of fact, I do."

We squeezed each other's hands conspiratorially. In a matter of moments, we'd slip out the back door.

Don't leave your own art opening! Karen would scold me.

Maybe it was a good thing she was back in Iowa, nursing twin boys—but then again, she wouldn't have expected me to take her advice anyway.

I looked up at Jason, and then nodded toward the emergency exit. He smiled.

I knew that nothing was certain. We'd have to see where things took us. But I knew that I wouldn't learn the end of our story tonight—and I hoped I wouldn't, not for a very long time.

THE LIFESAVER

James Patterson,
Frank Constantini,
and Brian Sitts

Chapter I

Near Wilmington, Mass., 12:15 a.m.

"Wow. I truly suck at this!"

Sorry, but that's my state of mind. If you were in my situation, you'd probably feel the same way. I'm in the living room sweating out my third novel—or my "third strike," as my publisher calls it. I guess that's only fair, considering my first two efforts pretty much ended up in the discount bin.

It's just past midnight, and I'm tapping away on my IBM Selectric. I realize that makes me look like a caveman with a sharp rock. No argument there. I've always been a little behind the times, technology-wise.

So I'm staring at the page. The words aren't coming. I feel burned out. Washed up. Useless.

I stand up to stretch. Other than another Red Sox pennant, there's only one thing that can make me feel better. Cuervo. I search the living room for a bottle I haven't drained yet. Suddenly—

thunka, thunka, thunka, thunka...

It's a crazy combination of whirring and pounding—coming from somewhere above me. My bookshelves start to rattle. I crouch my way to the front window.

I see a bright spotlight beam swinging across the roof of the Duffys' house next door. Treetops are bending like straws. The noise gets louder and louder. Closer and closer.

THUNKA, THUNKA, THUNKA!

I'm thinking terrorist attack, tornado, alien abduction... and I know it's not just the tequila. Whatever it is—it's real.

I'm squinting out the window, and I see a shape descending from the sky and setting down in the empty field on the other side of my house.

It's a helicopter! But not one of those chunky traffic choppers. This one is small, sleek, elegant. And now it's about fifty feet away from me, blowing the lids off my trash cans.

The rotor blades are still spinning. A guy hops out and ducks against the prop wash. He crosses the driveway and heads straight for my front door. I open it just as he's coming up my front steps. Whoever it is, he looks like he just stepped off a yacht. Or an ultra-cool helicopter.

"Mr. Crane? Damian Crane?"

I'm staring over the guy's shoulder at the chopper. My eyes are so wide I probably look like Bart Simpson.

"Right. Yes. That's me..."

The white strobe on the belly of the chopper is lighting up the ground in quick, bright blasts. Emergency landing? What else could it be?

"Everybody okay?" I ask. "Should I call 911?" But the guy is totally calm.

"No need," he says. "Everything is fine. Can we talk?"

The chopper engines are powering down. Good thing the neighbors are away. Mrs. Duffy throws a fit when I turn up my Beats on the porch. She'd have a stroke over this. The guy steps inside. Trim. Good-looking. But really pale. He gets right down to business. There's no mistake. It's me he's looking for.

"Mr. Crane," he says, "my name is Tyler Bron. I don't know if you've ever heard of me, but... I'm a computer engineer."

The name is quasi-familiar. Maybe from the business pages. Or CNN?

"I founded Bron Aerospace. That's my company."

Now it clicks. Tyler Bron. Bron Aerospace. Right. Shuttle supply missions, satellite communications, air force contracts—the works. That would explain the state-of-the-art transportation. And, by the way, "computer engineer" is underselling it just a bit. Tyler Bron is a certified Steve Jobs–level genius, not to mention a mega-billionaire. And for some reason, he's standing in my living room.

"Good to meet you. But please...call me Damian."

We shake hands. I toss aside a pile of notebooks and pizza boxes to clear some room for him to sit. Embarrassing. This guy's pants cost more than my sofa.

Bron is polite, but a little awkward and nervous. If I were describing him in a book, I'd say, "distracted." But the big questions are: What does he want with me? Why the hell is he here? He presses his palms together and starts in.

"First, Mr. Crane...Damian...I need to tell you that I'm a fan. I love everything you've ever written."

That's definitely a first for me.

"Oh—so you're the one," I say. I know, I know—obvious joke. But the thing is, it goes right past him. He's totally sincere—not bullshitting me in the least. He really seems to like my stuff. He starts quoting from *Esquire* pieces and newspaper profiles I wrote ten years ago—stuff I'd totally forgotten. Then he spills out his problem.

Turns out, he's done nothing but work since the day he dropped out of MIT to start his company. He's been on the job 24/7 since then. No rest. No vacations. No downtime. He's got more money than he'll ever need, but it doesn't mean anything to him anymore. He's got no time to enjoy it.

"The truth is, Damian, I've been starting to think about everything I don't have. No family, no friends, no personal relationships."

"I'm forty years old," he says, "and I have zero human connections. None."

I'm sitting there listening to his story—and I don't know what to say. I like the guy. I guess I feel sorry for him in a way, but what does any of this have to do with me? I'm no psychologist. I'm so nervous I blurt out the only comforting thing I can think of.

"Want a drink?"

I know I do.

He shakes his head. Then he leans forward.

"Damian, as I said . . . you're the best writer I know."

I'm still trying to absorb that unlikely fact. And now he lands the kicker:

"I want you to write me a life."

Chapter 2

*T*IME OUT. Now this is officially getting strange. A guy this rich needs a favor from me?

"Write you a life? Wait. You mean…you want me to put you in a novel?" That's not a problem. In my last book, I made my mailman a serial killer.

He shakes his head again.

"No. What I want, Damian, is for you to write a whole new existence for me. In the real world. Whatever you create on the page will happen in real life. I have people who can make it happen. Cost is no object. If you agree, my associate can be here in the morning to arrange everything."

Maybe I'm dense. This is not really computing in my feeble brain. But Bron is dead serious. And let's be honest. Look around. What have I got to lose?

"Hold on," I say. "For just one minute, let's pretend that this is even remotely possible. What kind of life would you want?"

Tyler Bron stands up and smiles, just a little.

"Surprise me."

Chapter 3

Bam! Bam! Bam!

Oh, God have mercy. My head is splitting. I'm crumpled on my sofa under a blanket, wondering if last night was some kind of hallucination.

Bam! Bam! Bam!

My front door again. Doorbell broken. Must...answer. I run my hands over my belly. Still wearing my Red Sox T-shirt. Briefs? Check. Just need to pull on my jeans. I stand up. Whoa there, cowboy! Dizzy...queasy...shaky. The trifecta.

BAM! BAM! BAM!

"Who the f—??! Coming!"
I lurch across the living room. What the hell time is it? Six a.m.!? Christ.

I open the front door, hoping it's a Jehovah's Witness I can yell at. Instead...

"Mr. Crane? I'm Daisy DeForest. Tyler Bron's associate. Mr. Bron said you'd be expecting me."

Business suit. Hair pulled back. Thirty-five, maybe. Attractive, if you like the buttoned-up type. But way too intense for this hour of the morning. I rub my eyes, trying hard to focus. Truth is, after last night, I don't know what to expect.

"Wow. Okay. I guess he wasn't kidding." I mumble my words, trying not to project too much. Right now, my breath would singe her eyebrows.

"No. He wasn't. Can we get started? We've got a lot to get through."

Quite the drill sergeant, this one.

"Now? Okay. Wait. So...I...what do I need...?"

"Nothing. Just you. Let's go."

I hold up my index finger in the universal sign for "wait a sec," and go back in to find my shoes. I pop into the bathroom for a hit of Listerine and smear on some deodorant. When I head back through the living room, my new best friend is already in her car, engine revving. A jet-black Audi RS 7.

First observation: Daisy does not drive like a daisy. She peels out of my driveway spitting gravel, and before I can blink we're on I-93, doing 95. She pulls up to within five inches of an eighteen-wheeler's backside before drafting around it, punching it up to 110 as she passes.

To be honest, I'm only guessing at the speed, because

I'm gripping the handhold for dear life and staring straight ahead. Conversation? Forget it. I'm just trying not to lose the mostly liquid contents of my stomach.

Somewhere near the New Hampshire border, we fly down an exit ramp and start winding down a back road like it's Le Mans. I spot a speed limit sign, but it's just a blur. Now we're turning into a private roadway. The speed bumps slow her down slightly. We pass a rough granite obelisk with BRON AEROSPACE etched into it. Impressive. Classy. Expensive.

Up ahead through the trees, I see a building—all glass and steel, with a front that looks like the prow of a sailing ship. Some pricey architect's wet dream. Daisy cruises into a turnaround right in front of the main entrance and turns off the engine. Guess she can park wherever she damn pleases.

The lobby goes up ten stories, with skylights that let you see clear into the clouds. Hanging there in the middle of all that open air is some kind of space contraption with antennas and probes and solar panels sticking out in every direction. Looks like a very expensive insect. Daisy sees me looking.

"The Bron-1. Our first. March 2002," says Daisy. "Tick, tock. Let's go."

So much for the guided tour. We walk up a floating staircase to the mezzanine level. The whole place is buzzing with young techies. They're all wearing jeans and T-shirts. Like me, only ten times hipper. In fact, I feel totally out of place. Daisy stands out from the crowd, too—and not just because of how she's dressed. They're kids. She's a grown-up.

Now we're in a conference room looking out over the atrium. Daisy pulls some papers from a binder and slides them across the table to me. For the next five minutes, I'm scrawling my name across legal documents. Confidentiality agreement. Indemnification policy. Liability waiver. You name it.

After every swipe of the pen, Daisy whacks a heavy-duty stamp onto the page. DAISY DEFOREST, PH.D. / ATTY. AT LAW.

Overachiever.

And now she's starting in with the technical stuff, reeling off terms I don't even remotely understand. Firewalls. Encryption codes. Authentication protocols. I'm pretending to pay attention. Truly I am. I'm looking right at her. I'm hearing her words. But she might as well be speaking Inuit.

Now she's laying out the ground rules. One: We have no contact with Tyler Bron. Two: Whatever I create, Daisy and her team will make it come to life, no limitations. Three: She handles logistics, transport, communications, everything. All I do is write. My head is spinning. My guts are still churning. Then she slides a sleek new silver laptop across the table. Looks about as thin as a bar coaster.

"This is the only one of its kind in the world. I had our techs tweak it just for you. It's got everything you need, and more."

This is a problem. She's talking to a guy who still has a flip phone. I'm embarrassed, but I try not to show it. I stare at the laptop and give Daisy the bad news.

"Sorry, I can't write on that thing."

"I don't understand. You use a tablet?"

"I use a typewriter."

This stops her for a second. She wrinkles her nose. I can see her brain whirring, trying to make sense of it.

"A typewriter. You mean like in *All the President's Men*?"

"No. Not a manual typewriter. A Selectric. Very different."

Daisy rubs her brow like she has a headache. And obviously, the headache is me. Not that she cares, but the feeling is definitely mutual. She takes a deep breath and gives me a tight little smile.

"Okay, then," she says, "we'll have to do a work-around for that."

The drive back to my house is even faster—if that's possible. I'm still a little wobbly when I climb out of the car. Daisy leans toward the passenger side window and calls after me: "Mr. Crane! Be ready tomorrow: 5:00 a.m. Packed. With your...machine. In the meantime, start writing."

Start writing. Okay. So, I've got till 5:00 a.m. to give a guy I just met a fresh start on a life he never had. No problem.

Daisy starts to pull away. I wave my arms to stop her.

"Hold it! Wait! What climate should I pack for?"

Seems like a reasonable question. But Daisy shakes

her head like I'm the puppy who keeps peeing on her rug.

"You're still not getting this, are you?"

"Getting what?"

"It's your choice, Mr. Crane. It's all on you. Whatever you write, that's where we're going."

Chapter 4

Unknown, 6:00 a.m.

Dawn in the desert. A two-lane blacktop cuts through nothing but sand, rocks, and scrubby brush. A black Suburban comes over a rise and pulls onto the shoulder. The left rear passenger door opens. A man steps out. The Suburban takes off and disappears into the distance.

Tyler Bron blinks against the morning sun and turns in a slow circle. No idea where he is. He reaches for his iPhone. Google Maps will clear this up. Uh-oh. No phone. He does a quick pat-down of all his pockets. His heart starts pounding. Not only no phone . . . no wallet. No cards. No keys. No cash. Nothing. Crane, he thinks, you've really done it.

Wait . . . in his right rear pants pocket, he finds something. A folded piece of paper. He pulls it out and opens it. It has five words on it, in a typewriter font:

`Welcome to your new life.`

Chapter 5

DAMN IT'S hot! Still early morning, But Bron is already sweating through the back of his shirt. He scans the horizon in every direction. Nothing. Okay, Tyler, make a decision. The sun is there. That's east. So the road runs north–south. Pick a direction. Flip a coin. Oh…right. No coins. Then north it is. He starts walking.

Bron feels like his brain is frying. He's wondering how Crane knew there's nothing he hates worse than sun and heat—or was it just a lucky guess? "Well," Bron says to himself, "I asked for a new life. Let's hope it gets better than this."

Grandpa Alvarez is singing along to a Hispanic pop station in his 1998 F-150. His grandson, Gonzalo, is on the bench seat beside him. Since Gonzalo's parents died, this ten-year-old has been the light of his grandfather's life. It's just the two of them against the world. Three—if you count Gonzalo's pet rooster, sitting calmly on the skinny boy's lap.

Gonzalo is the first to spot the speck in the road ahead.

"¡Mira! ¿Qué es esso?"

Grandpa stops mid-verse and squints. Unbelievable. What kind of *idiota* would be alone on the road out here? He looks for an abandoned vehicle. Nothing. They get closer. A hiker? No way. Not dressed like that.

Bron hears the hum of the pickup before he sees it. And now that it's approaching, he does something he's seen only in pictures: he sticks out his thumb.

The truck pulls off onto the shoulder. The passenger door creaks open. Bron slides onto the bench seat, squeezing Gonzalo into the middle, closer to his *abuelo.* Bron exhales a breath of relief.

"Thanks," he says, wiping the sweat from his forehead. "Thanks very much."

"De nada," says the boy. "I'm Gonzalo. That's my grandpa."

"I'm Tyler. Nice to meet you both."

The bird offers a guttural cluck.

Grandpa looks down at Bron's black Ferragamo loafers, now coated with a fine film of dust. He starts laughing.

"¡Loco!" says grandpa. *"¡Una serpiente de cascabel picaría a través de sus zapatillas!"*

Bron is fluent in Mandarin, but that won't help him here. Gonzalo translates:

"Grandpa says a rattlesnake would bite right through your slippers."

Terrific. Bron knows the great outdoors was never his strong suit. For the past twenty years, his climate has been hermetically controlled, along with everything else in his life. He feels like all his senses are blasting on full alert for the first time in a long time. Maybe ever.

The blazing white sand. The smell of gasoline and stale sweat. The throbbing heat in the cab of the truck. The rush of hot air from the open windows.

And then there's that bird. Big. Ugly. Menacing. It looks Bron up and down with black, beady eyes.

"Nice chicken," Bron says to Gonzalo.

"Cock," says Gonzalo. "His name is Zapata. Go ahead. You can pet him."

On the list of things Bron wants to do right now, this is dead last. He extends his hand slowly. Zapata's head swivels like a dashboard ornament.

Suddenly the bird lets out an unearthly squawk and drives his beak toward Bron's extended fingers. Bron pulls away sharply, a nanosecond from getting seriously pecked. Damn it! An attack rooster!

Gonzalo tugs the surly bird back into his lap. "No! *¡Malo Zapata!* That's no way to treat a guest!"

Grandpa turns the radio back up and begins to hum along to a Spanish pop song. Bron tries to ask Grandpa a question above the music.

"Excuse me? Hey! Señor! Where am I?"

This much English, Grandpa understands.

"En el medio de la nada," he says, chuckling. Bron looks to Gonzalo for the translation.

Two words:

"You're nowhere."

Chapter 6

*H*ow is this happening? It's way beyond me, and it's making my head spin.

I'm sitting in a huge, climate-controlled hangar just a few miles away, seeing this whole scene play out almost as if I were inside the pickup. I'm watching it all on a sports bar–size screen, and every word is crystal clear.

"Boost the resolution a little," says Daisy to one of her techs. She's standing at a console under the big screen — totally on her game, and totally ignoring me.

I can see that Bron is anxious — and really sweaty. I feel kind of guilty sitting here nibbling M&M's. But not really. He's the one who wanted a change, right? So I decided to swing for the fences. And true to her word, Daisy is making it happen.

I wrote the most remote location I could think of, and there it is — for real — right before my eyes.

I admit, the three hours I spent in the back of the cargo plane last night were a little bumpy. Not exactly first-class accommodations. But everything got here in one piece. Me. Daisy. A bunch of hi-tech whiz kids. And a pile of complicated electronic stuff—plus my trusty Selectric, safe and sound.

From the outside, the hangar looks like it has gone through a nuclear bomb test. But inside, I have to say, Daisy and her minions have done it up nice. Blond wood tables, glass desks, slick workstations. Even a few sofas and some semi-comfortable sleeping cubicles. Our own little world in the middle of the desert.

"Got everything you need, sir?" asks one of the techies.

"I could use a beer."

"It's 10:00 a.m.," says Daisy from a few yards away. Point taken.

She must have bought out eBay's backlog of Selectric typewriter ribbon, because I've got about twenty extra cartridges stacked in a box by my desk. Not to mention five reams of twenty-pound extra-white typing paper. Enough for a few novels. Or one new life. Which is why we're here—why I wrote Bron here. Way out of his comfort zone. Way out of mine.

In fashion news…Daisy has ditched the business suit for tight black jeans and a Bron Aerospace polo shirt. Change in look, but not in attitude. In fact, she's already told me to stop asking questions. Twice. I don't know why, but something about her makes me want to press her buttons.

"Drones—am I right? We're using drones!" I ask. A guy has a right to be curious.

"Switch to vector two point four," she tells the tech. It's like I'm not even here.

We watch Grandpa make a turn from one dusty, god-forsaken road onto another. Then she turns to me.

"Don't worry about it," she says. "Not your arena. Just keep writing."

She wiggles her fingers at me like typing.

"Let's go, Shakespeare. What happens next?"

Chapter 7

GRANDPA BOUNCES over a deep rut in the road. Zapata squawks, and Bron nearly bounces into the roof of the truck cab. A sharp turn tosses him against the door. The windshield is covered with a thick layer of dust. Grandpa hits the washer button. The wipers clear an arc in front of Bron just as the truck slows down and pulls into a small town. No warning. No signs. Suddenly, it's just there.

Actually, "town" is an exaggeration. It's more like a settlement — an odd assortment of low stucco and adobe buildings in the middle of an ocean of sand.

But compared to the last fifty miles, it's a metropolis. It's civilization. And Tyler Bron, micromanager, is ready to take control of his situation. He's always been able to make things work. Why should this place be any different?

Grandpa pulls into a gas station with a single pump and a one-bay repair shop.

"Pit stop?" asks Bron.

"Nope," says Gonzalo. "Home."

Bron looks around. No way.

"Gonzalo, I need a favor. Can I borrow your cell phone?" Gonzalo shrugs as he sets Zapata down on the ground. The bird starts pecking the sand.

"No cell phones, señor," says Gonzalo. "No service."

Grandpa grips the pump handle as he fuels up the truck. Bron looks over and mimes holding a phone to his ear. Grandpa shakes his head and laughs.

"Are you kidding me?" Bron says. "This is unbelievable." How much worse can it get?

"No cable, either," says Gonzalo.

This is officially Bron's worst nightmare: a world he can't control with a keypad. He truly feels like he's on a different planet. He needs a way to get his bearings again. Some way to manage things. Think!

Bron scans up and down the dusty main street. Butch and Sundance would feel totally at home here. Beyond the garage, he can see a bar, a diner, a hardware store, a stucco schoolhouse, and not much else.

Grandpa's finished gassing up. He opens the door to the pickup, reaches behind the seat, and pulls out a battered straw sombrero. He tosses it to Bron like a Frisbee. Bron reaches, but misses. The sombrero lands in the dust.

"¡El sol se hará perder la cabeza!"

Gonzalo picks up the hat and hands it to Bron. "He says, 'The sun will make you crazy.'"

"I think I might be crazy already," says Bron. He could be sitting in his cool air-conditioned office right now, sipping a mineral water. What the hell has he gotten himself into?

Bron puts the hat on. Even his shadow looks ridiculous. But it offers a little shade for his eyes. He squints toward the edge of town and sees a building with faux pillars and gold gilt lettering on the window. A bank! Definitely not one of those too-big-to-fail banks—but still, a bank. Banks have money. And money, Bron thinks to himself, can fix just about anything.

He heads down the street, looking like one of the Three Amigos.

Inside the bank, manager Domingo Sanchez is filing papers. His teller, Maria, is filing her nails, bored out of her mind. It's just the two of them. No customers yet.

Sanchez is looking prosperous. For him, banking is serious business, and he makes it a point to dress the part in a dark blue three-piece suit—even on days like this, when the heat makes him sweat through all three pieces.

Sanchez looks up as Bron walks through the door. The manager jumps up, suddenly energized. He snaps his fingers at Maria, who quickly drops the nail file into a pencil cup and sits up straight in her teller's chair. Sanchez tugs his vest hem down over his belly and turns on his most welcoming smile.

"*Buenos días.* Good morning, sir! Domingo Sanchez, bank manager. How may I be of service today?"

Bron whips off the goofy sombrero and looks around. Two standard Steelcase desks. A few file cabinets. And a vault that says (no kidding), Acme Safe Company. But a bank is a bank, right? A bank can connect with other banks. Money can be wired. And money can put Bron right back where he's used to being—in charge.

"Yes. Good morning. I need to access my accounts, please."

Sanchez dabs a patch of sweat from his high forehead with a handkerchief. He beams. "Of course, of course, sir. And your accounts are currently located... where?"

"At Chase Bank. In Massachusetts."

"Massachusetts. You're quite a ways from home, then. Vacation?"

"Right," says Bron, "let's go with that."

"Well, that's fine, fine. No problem at all, Mister...?"

"Bron. Tyler Bron." He wonders for a millisecond if his name might ring a bell. But nothing.

Sanchez motions toward a chair in front of his tidy desk. "Mister Bron. Please."

Bron sits. Sanchez takes a seat behind the desk and straightens two thick pens in front of him, ready for business.

"All right then, Mr. Bron. First things first. All I need are two forms of ID."

ID? Oh, shit.

Chapter 8

SOMEWHERE, THOUSANDS of miles away, there are bank and brokerage accounts in Tyler Bron's name, with ten juicy digits in the balance columns. Billions, just sitting there. But here, Bron is experiencing something he's never felt in his life. The feeling of being a nobody.

It's not a great feeling.

Bron steps out of the bank into the blinding sun, trying to adjust to the notion of being practically penniless. He spots Gonzalo riding his battered two-wheeler down the middle of the street. Gonzalo spots Bron and skids to a stop, kicking up a cloud of dust. He reads Bron's expression.

"*¿Qué pasa?*" says Gonzalo. "*¿No dinero?*"

Bron jerks his thumb back toward the bank. "You know Mister Sanchez?"

"Señor Sanchez? Sí."

"Well, he's a real stickler for rules."

Bron tugs out the lining of his pockets like a clown. At least he's trying to keep a sense of humor about it. If he expected a challenge, Crane has definitely delivered. But what now? He can't hike out of here. He'd be buzzard meat within an hour. So, what now?

"You need a place to stay—no money?" asks Gonzalo.

Bron thinks for a second. "You know a place?"

Gonzalo pops a wheelie and circles his hand in the air, like Lawrence of Arabia leading a charge.

"Señor! This way!"

The town motel is located a block beyond the gas station, tucked behind a small warehouse. It's just a one-room office with seven tiny units lined up across a tiled courtyard. Decades of desert sun have faded the colors to pale pastels. A wooden walkway runs in front of the units, widening in the center to a common deck with a few lounge chairs and umbrellas.

The Four Seasons, it's not.

Gonzalo lays his bike down and waits for Bron to catch up. Bron rounds the corner and looks up at a blinking neon sign, Motel Alvarez. Below it is a wooden panel with a single word: VACANCY.

Gonzalo holds the door open. Bron walks into the dimly lit office. The manager is at the front desk, leaning casually on a dog-eared leather register.

Of course. It figures.

Hello again . . . Grandpa.

Chapter 9

O H, MY God!"

Who knew a simple shower could feel this good? Bron turns slowly under the flow as sweat and sand wash out of his hair and every remote nook and cranny of his body. The pipes creak and the water never gets past lukewarm, but no matter. Right now, lukewarm is heaven. Worth every penny of the forty-dollar-per-night room fee, reluctantly waived by Grandpa—but only until Bron can dig up some actual cash. Worry about that later. For now, this is bliss.

As Bron steps out of the shower, there's a knock on the door. He wraps a towel around his waist and peeks out through the peephole. It's Gonzalo, bearing gifts.

"¡Hola, Señor Tyler!"

Through the half-open door, Gonzalo hands Bron a pair of faded cargo shorts and a few STP T-shirts. Then a pair of rubber sandals.

"Hope they fit," says Gonzalo.

"Thanks, Gonzalo. They'll be fine. Really. Thank you."

"Give me your clothes," says Gonzalo. "I'll get them cleaned for you."

Bron wraps his sweaty slacks, shirt, briefs, and socks in an extra towel and hands them over. Gonzalo tucks the packet under his arm and runs toward the office building. He calls back, "Ready *mañana*! On the house!"

Bron has never been crazy about kids. They've always made him uncomfortable. But he has to admit, this one is a real find.

He slips on the shorts and T-shirt, hangs up the wet towel, and flops onto the bed for the only thing better than a nice warm shower—a nice long nap.

His eyes close…he starts to drift off…Minutes pass… maybe hours…

And then, suddenly:

"All I do is WIN, WIN, WIN…!"

The pumping sound of DJ Khaled wakes Bron with a start. And it's not just the music. It's the sound of two strong male voices singing along with gusto. The bed is so close to the window, Bron can roll over and peek through the blind slats.

"What the…?"

The music is blaring from the deck out front. Sitting there in facing lounge chairs are two guys in bathing suits, shirts open, both wearing Ray-Bans. On the deck between them is a portable speaker connected to an iPhone. Resting on their chests—outrageously large cocktails. In the real world, Bron would think about picking up the phone to complain about the noise. But this is not the real world. Also, there's no phone.

Bron emerges tentatively from his room, rubbing his eyes against the late afternoon glare. The two guys look up and whip off their sunglasses at the same time.

"Oh, no!" says one. "We are so rude!"

"Wow. Sorry. We didn't realize there was anybody else here!" adds the other. "Apologies for the concert. Really, man...so sorry."

Bron's fellow guests look like a pair of All-American quarterbacks—with a swagger to match. They're immediately friendly, charming, and irresistible—totally comfortable in their own skin. From the look of them, they appear to have life figured out. Even here.

"Don't worry about it," says Bron. "I'm Tyler."

"I'm Timo," says the one with the blond crew cut and the elaborate angel tat on his chest.

"Luke," says the one with the artfully shaved dome. He points to his nearly empty glass. "Drink?"

Bron can still feel the road dust in the back of his throat. He pulls an extra chair from his room onto the deck. "Sure," he says. "Why not?"

Luke rolls out of his lounge chair and gestures toward the end of the row. "Tyler, allow me to escort you to libation central!"

Weaving a bit, Luke leads the way to Unit 1. He opens the door and waves Bron in. "After you, sir..."

The room is a mirror image of Bron's, but with one major addition. Sitting on the dresser is a world-class, kick-ass margarita machine. Luke pats it lovingly.

"We don't go anywhere without it."

As Luke dumps a bucketful of ice cubes into the stainless-steel contraption, Bron glances over at the bed. In a room this small, there's no way to miss it. Rumpled and slept in—with two pairs of guys' jeans lying on top of the sheets. Okay. Got it.

After the ice, Luke dumps in what looks like an entire fifth of Patrón. Then a whole bottle of bright green liquid. He presses a button. The room lights dim for a second.

"Go, baby!" says Luke, rubbing the machine like a genie's bottle.

The device gives off a powerful grinding noise that quickly evens out to a loud hum. Luke steadies the heavy-duty glass pitcher as it fills with a greenish slurry. He shouts above the sound . . .

"What brings you here, Tyler?"

Bron shouts back. "Long story."

"No kidding. Same here. We were on our way to the coast. Transmission blew. Car's in the shop down the street—waiting for parts."

"Could be a long wait."

"Tell me about it. Ten days far. And . . . here we are!"

Bron and Luke rejoin Timo on the deck, all three now equipped with super-size beverages. Luke hoists his glass: "To strangers in a strange land." Clinks all around.

Bron puts the glass to his lips and tastes his first blast of the concoction: killer sweet and sledgehammer strong. It tastes soooo good—ice and booze blended to a frosty citrus slush. He should sip, but he slurps.

"What business you in, Tyler?" asks Timo.

"Computers," Bron says. Close enough. And at the moment, nobody seems all that interested in career résumés anyway.

"That's cool," says Timo, lowering his shades.

"Very cool," says Luke, doing the same.

Bron tucks his feet under his chair. Suddenly he feels a slithery touch just below his ankle. He leaps up, spilling half his drink and knocking his chair back. A tiny lizard skitters from under the chair and off across the deck. Luke and Timo tilt their sunglasses up and watch the critter disappear around the corner.

"Western whiptail!" shouts Luke.

"No way," says Timo. "That's a desert spiny."

"Whiptail."

"You're nuts! Spiny!"

Back and forth they go, laughing. Whiptail. Spiny. Whiptail. Spiny. Bron rights his chair and settles back down, his brain becoming comfortably numb. His head is swimming with the booze and the great lizard debate and, in a nonsensical way, how good it all feels. Warm. Relaxing. Friendly. Before he knows it, there's a refill in his glass. Then another. Jesus.

Hours pass. As the shadows deepen, strings of multi-colored year-round Christmas lights pop on, outlining buildings and fences up and down the street. Kind of pretty, especially because it's all kind of blurry. The last thing Bron sees is Luke and Timo doing drunken hip-hop moves on the deck. The last thing he hears is the pounding of the music from the speaker:

Got money on my mind, I can never get enough...

Chapter 10

TYLER BRON is 170 pounds of dead weight—out cold and snoring. Timo holds his ankles, Luke has him under the armpits. They carry him the ten yards back to his room and set him gently on the bed. Luke slips Bron's sandals off and places them neatly on the floor.

"I wasn't planning on this part," says Timo.

"I'm not the one who mixed the drinks," says Luke.

They head toward the door, but Timo has a thought. He goes back and rolls Bron onto his side. "Just in case he pukes," he whispers. Luke gives a quick thumbs-up. They slip out and close the door softly.

As they walk down the wooden walkway toward their room, hands on each other's shoulders, Luke says, "Okay, he's down. Are we done?"

But . . . he's not talking to Timo or to anybody else in sight. He's talking into thin air. But talking to whom?

Chapter 11

SPOOKY. REALLY spooky.

I'm watching a hi-def feed from a camera on the motel deck. Everything's in night-vision mode now. Very *Zero Dark Thirty*. Luke and Timo look like two glowing ghosts moving along the porch toward their room.

Daisy is standing near the monitor, wearing a nearly invisible Bluetooth headset. As usual, she does the talking.

"That's it for tonight, guys. Thanks."

I give myself a little pat on the back. God knows I won't get one from her. I have to admit, Luke and Timo are perfect. Daisy couldn't have done a better job with the casting. Now Tyler Bron has a couple of bros—just the way I wrote them.

Chapter 12

*D*AMN, THAT'S good weed!

The trim brunette in a peasant skirt leans against a stucco wall outside her place of employment, which is definitely a smoke-free environment. It's a beautiful day, and getting mellower by the minute. She looks up into the cloudless sky, takes another deep drag, then exhales an impressive plume, which is carried away on a light desert breeze.

Whoa. Not too much now. Need to be on point. But the sky is so beautiful...

Ding, ding, ding!

Shit! It's the bell from inside. She takes a final puff, stubs out the joint carefully against the wall and sticks it in her pocket. She brushes her hands briskly over her top and skirt to make sure no ashes linger, then straightens her name tag.

WILLOW BAILEY, LIBRARIAN.

Inside, Tyler wanders past neat rows of wooden card

catalogs and stacks of neatly filed books. In a tiny space labeled KID'S CORNER, colorful beanbag chairs surround a low table scattered with oversize picture books and stuffed animals. Bron's head is still throbbing from last night, but this morning he's a man on a mission. He calls out toward the back of the room . . .

"Hello? Anybody here?"

Willow pushes open the door from the back hall, shifting back, shifting back into professional mode.

"Sorry, sorry, it's just me today," she calls out. And then, as she rounds the corner into the main room, "Hi, there. I'm Willow. I'm the librarian."

Okay, Bron thinks to himself, this is no dowdy book checker. Young, hip, cute. Maybe a little . . . spacey.

Okay, Willow thinks to herself, this is no local cowboy. Tall, polite, attractive. Definitely a little . . . sunburned.

"How can I help?" asks Willow. "Looking for anything special?"

"Hi. I'm Tyler. I just got here yesterday, and to tell the truth, I'm not even sure *how* I got here, but anyway . . . I need some help connecting with the world."

"Oh," says Willow, "like . . . self-help?" She brightens. Right up her alley. "Chakras? Meridians? Inner power? That sort of thing?"

"No, no. I mean connecting. Actually connecting . . . digitally."

"Oh." Willow's expression falls just a little.

"Please tell me you have a computer," Bron says.

Willow recovers and gives Bron a don't-be-silly look. "Of course we have a computer. It's in the back…"

They walk past a row of well-worn encyclopedias and a wooden pedestal holding a huge Spanish–English dictionary. Following a step behind, Bron can't help but notice the sway of Willow's hips. And her bare feet. And the rings on her toes. Making small talk with attractive young women has never been Bron's forte, but he gives it a shot.

"Can I ask you something?" Bron says.

"Sure."

"What's the story with this town? Is it actually on the map? Does it even have a name?"

"Nada."

"Nada? Nothing? You mean…it doesn't have a name?"

"No, I mean Nada is the name. Before 1940, this was just desert. Then they started mining for uranium here, for the Manhattan Project. They put up some Quonset huts, built a few buildings and bars and some hangars outside of town. Thing is, they never found any uranium. Not a speck. So the scientists called the place "Nada." Their little joke. These days, nobody really calls it anything. It just kind of…is."

Willow stops at a small study carrel in the back of the room and makes an adorably awkward "ta-dah" motion. Behold…the computer! A Dell desktop model—from the mid-1990s. The boxy monitor sits on top of a CPU with two slots for floppy disks. Over nearly three decades, the cabinet and keyboard have gone from beige to brownish. A museum piece for sure.

"Wow," says Bron, "I think I used one of these once...
in high school."

"Well," says Willow, "it doesn't get a lot of use here. So
I'm sure it's good as new."

The space is tight, but even so, Willow is standing a
little bit closer than necessary. Bron can smell the fra-
grance of herbal shampoo radiating from her hair. And
something else? Can't be. He must be imagining it.

"All right then," says Willow, clapping her palms
together. "I will leave you to it!"

"Do I need a password?" Bron asks.

"Nope. Already logged in."

Bron sits down at the ancient machine and clicks the
only browser icon on the screen: AOL.

Nothing. Then... *Sssssssssssssss Boing, Boing, Boing! Click.*

"Dial up. Of course," Bron mutters to himself.

Somehow, back at her desk, Willow overhears him.

"Need help with the technology back there?"

"Nope," Bron calls back, "I think I've got it."

The download time is glacial. Excruciating. Ten whole
minutes for Bron to view his company website, where
he discovers that he has taken a leave of absence.

He taps out the password for his company email.
"Address disabled." He tries Google Mail. His account is
gone—vaporized. Same with LinkedIn, bank and brokerage passwords. Everything.

Impressive, Bron thinks. Crane has really thought of
everything. In the digital universe, Tyler Bron no longer
exists. No timeline. No profiles. No history. Just the now.

He rolls back in the chair and lets out a long breath. His old world is gone, but what's left? When he asked Crane to write him a life, this is not what he had in mind. Not by a long shot.

Willow is at the front desk reading a reflexology book as Bron emerges from the back.

"All good?" she asks.

"Well," says Bron, "I learned some things about myself."

"Good for you," she says. "Namaste."

Just as he reaches the door, Bron has a thought. He turns. Willow looks up and smiles. Pretty.

"One more question. Have you read any books by an author named Damian Crane?"

Willow gives it some thought, then shakes her head. "Nope. Sorry. Never heard of him."

Chapter 13

SONOVABITCH! GODDAMN hi-tech crap!"

Pico Fuentes, proprietor of Pico's Auto Repair & Body Shop, is pissed off big-time. He heaves a repair manual into the wall on the other side of the garage, barely missing the passion-red Mazda in the repair bay.

Pico is sixty-five and feeling every day of it. He's old enough to remember when cars were really cars, with vent windows and ashtrays and hood ornaments... and carburetors. He really misses carburetors. Now it's all electronic fuel injection, oxygen sensors, and on-board diagnostic protocols. He's got the hood open on a 2006 Dodge Dakota and he might as well be staring into the goddamn space shuttle.

The last thing he needs right now is visitors. But he's about to get some.

Oh, no. Please. Not again. They're back. And now with a third one?

"Pico, my man! *¿Qué pasa?*" calls Luke.

"We're here to check on the patient!" says Timo.

Today, for the first time, Bron tags along. It's his first

visit to Pico's since he rolled into town with Grandpa and Gonzalo two weeks ago. Seems like about two light-years.

As Bron steps into the garage with his buddies, he gets smacked with the odors of grease and oil and, to be blunt...of Pico. The temperature in the shop is pushing ninety, and those overalls haven't seen the inside of a washing machine in a while. Pico is a big guy with a burly beard. Reminds Bron of a pre-diet Zac Brown. But a lot less cuddly.

"See for yourself," says Pico with a snarl. He waves a meaty hand toward the drive train and rear differential on the floor.

"Your toy isn't gonna fix itself. I still need parts. And the boys over in Miyoshi are taking their sweet time."

"Almost a month now, Pico! How much longer?" asks Timo.

Pico shrugs. "Talk to Tojo."

Luke walks over to the Miata and runs his hands soothingly over the hood. "Patience, baby, patience..."

"You boys can stroke your sweetheart for as long as you want," says Pico, "but I got an emergency case here." He opens the door to the Dakota and turns the ignition switch. A sad little click comes from the engine compartment.

"Damn it!"

Pico grabs a hand-held engine analyzer off his work-table and leans under the steering column to find the data port. With his bulk, it's not a pretty sight. He's breathing hard. Sweating hard. He extracts himself from the cab with a mighty heave, grunting like a walrus. He stares at the readout and tugs at his beard like he's trying to pull it off.

"This code makes no goddamn sense!"

Bron is transfixed by the analyzer. His brain is alive and firing. This is the first piece of true twenty-first century technology he's seen in two weeks. He feels compelled to touch it.

"Mind if I take a look?" he blurts out.

Pico gives the pale gringo a dubious stare. "You know trucks, amigo?"

"I know electronics . . . a bit."

With a suspicious look, Pico hands over the greasy device. Bron takes the unit eagerly and presses a few buttons. He walks to the front of the truck and instinctively grabs a socket wrench. He hesitates, then nods toward the engine.

"Do you mind?" he asks.

"Go nuts," Pico says, "but if you fry anything, it's your ass."

Bron leans over the engine compartment. With a deft touch he unbolts a black plastic dust cover, exposing three huge plastic connectors, each with a thick bundle of multicolored wires. Bron pops the connectors free one at a time.

He studies the wiring pattern, his mind clicking a million miles an hour. He follows a red wire as thin as a blood vessel. He pulls a pen out of his pocket and probes gently into a tiny socket. He plugs the wiring connectors back in with three satisfying snaps. He turns his head to the side and calls to Pico.

"Try it now."

Pico reaches inside the cab and cranks the ignition key. The engine fires up. Luke and Timo lean back on the Miata and applaud.

"Bad connection in the PCU," Bron says. "The analyzers don't always pick it up." He closes the hood. "My name's Tyler, by the way."

"Drinking buddy of ours," says Timo, proudly.

"Well, I say he's a goddamn wizard," says Pico. He looks at Bron. "Appreciate the help."

Luke gives the Miata one last pat. "Okay. Show's over. Let's get a beer." Bron, Luke, and Timo head out of the garage. "Put a rush on those parts, okay, Pico?"

"Like I told you—I already did."

"Then maybe put a rush on the rush."

"Maybe next time, buy American," says Pico. Then, "Hey…Tyler." Bron stops and turns.

"You looking for a job?" Pico wipes his hands with a greasy rag. "I could use somebody who knows these goddamn computers. The pay sucks and so do the hours."

Tyler starts to laugh—but wait a minute. He now owes Grandpa about six hundred bucks for lodging, not counting the complementary breakfasts. He's been letting Luke and Timo pay for sandwiches and beer, along with depleting their supply of tequila and margarita mix.

This is crazy, Bron thinks. *I've never worked for anybody in my life. Never even applied for a job.*

But the thing is...he actually needs the money. He can't believe what he's saying until he actually hears the words come out of his mouth: "Absolutely. When do I start?"

Chapter 14

The next night

Tyler peels off his overalls and hangs them on a hook behind the office door. He scrubs as much of the grease off his hands and forearms as he can in the utility sink and heads out of the garage. He presses the button of the heavy overhead door so that it closes behind him, leaving a solitary work light casting a dim glow over tool chests and the still-dismantled Miata.

One oxygen sensor replacement. Two power-train control module adjustments. And three old-fashioned oil changes. Not a bad day's effort. And it actually felt good to work with his hand instead of his head for a change.

It's eight o'clock. The Christmas lights are on up and down the street, but Bron heads for the brightest light around—the neon sign over the Desert Diner, smack in the middle of town. His stomach is growling—and with a cash advance from Pico on his eleven-dollars-an-hour wages, the billionaire can finally pay for his own dinner.

The diner is small—about the length of a train car, with a row of booths along the window side and a counter facing the kitchen. Nothing here has been updated since the 1950s, except the jukebox in the far corner, which was updated a couple of decades later. Mixed in with the sound of clanking plates and the buzz of conversation, Bron can make out the bouncy chorus of "Bad, Bad Leroy Brown."

The place is packed. In fact, it looks like just about everybody in town is here. The handwritten sign up front reads, PLEASE SEAT YOURSELF. WE'LL FIND YOU EVENTU-ALLY. Bron takes a small table just inside the door, which gives him a view down the entire length of the place.

Maria the bank teller is moonlighting—waiting tables down at the other end. Her bank boss is at one of the counter stools, leaning over a bowl of chili. Grandpa is holding court with a posse of other guys in their seventies. Lots of laughing. Not many teeth. Grandpa sees Bron and tips his beer. Bron nods and raises his water glass, which is the only thing on his table at the moment.

Just as he turns to see if there's anybody around to help him out, a waitress spins out of the kitchen, grabs a laminated menu, and plops it in front of him. She's moving so fast she's a blur in his peripheral view. But even so, Bron can tell she's somebody he's never seen before.

"Thanks," he says, "I was just about to—"

"Order up!" The cook yells from the smoky kitchen as he pushes two heaping plates onto the pass. Now the jumpy waitress is torn: pick up the waiting food or take Bron's order. She glances at the sweaty cook, who wears a red bandana across his forehead like a pirate. He gives her a death stare.

No contest.

"Sorry, sorry," she says to Bron. "Be right back, I promise!" She's calling over her shoulder as she heads for the waiting food, and in one blink, Bron takes a mental snapshot so vivid he could describe her to a police sketch artist.

Late twenties. Long legs and a short black skirt. Dark blond hair pulled back into a ponytail with a few crazy-wild tendrils. Dark eyebrows that almost meet in the middle. And bright blue eyes.

He'd have a harder time describing the feeling in his gut. Hunger pangs? Nope. Something else.

Bron watches as she picks up the plates and quickly delivers them to the wrong booth. Then to a second booth. Wrong again. Finally, she gets it right. Third time's the charm. Shaking her head and blushing, she heads back to Bron's table and pulls out her order pad, which sends her pen flying onto the napkin holder. Bron hands the pen back to her.

"Thanks. Sorry. So sorry. It's only my second night."

In a movie, this is where Bron would have a witty comeback—a charming remark to make the pretty waitress feel that she's found a kindred spirit, a fellow outcast, some relief from the loneliness in this empty one-horse town.

But that doesn't happen. Not even close. Because Bron can hardly put two words together. This whole time, he hasn't even looked down at the menu. Because he's been looking at her.

"I . . . well," he stammers, "what do you recommend?"

She leans close, pretending to write on her pad. "Is he looking?"

"Who?"

"Kevin. The cook. Is he looking?"

"Nope. He's cooking."

She talks fast in a low voice:

"Okay. Listen. You seem new. And I want you to come back. So I'll give it to you straight. Burgers are fine. Stay away from the baked ham, which I think is actually Spam. Avoid anything with red sauce unless you like leftovers. Fries are so-so. Milk shakes are great. Pies are excellent, especially the coconut cream. If you want dessert, I would order it with your meal, because I might forget to ask you later."

"Fair enough," says Bron. He orders a burger, fries, a milk shake, and the pie.

When his food arrives a few minutes later, it's just as she promised. The burger is juicy and tasty. The fries are fine. The milk shake is creamy and smooth. And the pie—well, he's never had better.

He finishes his dinner and sips his water. He thinks

about ordering coffee. But he's not about to add more pressure. This girl looks like she could crack at any minute.

"How was everything?"

Now she's reaching across him to clear his plates. Up close, he can see a sprinkle of freckles across her cheeks. Her arm accidently brushes his shoulder. She smells like lemons. He's searching for something memorable to say.

"Compliments to the chef," is all he can come up with. Weak.

"Let's not give him a swelled head," she says.

"No thanks. I'm good." Give it up. Cut your losses.

She rips the check from her pad and puts it face-down on the edge of the table.

"Order up!" The pirate calls. And she's gone, backing away. "Have a good night," she says.

Bron turns the check over. Under the item prices and circled total, there's a scrawled signature, "Sunny," with a little smiley face.

Sitting alone in his booth, Tyler Bron actually smiles back at it.

Chapter 15

Ten miles away

Nailed it. Enough for one day.

I switch off the Selectric and roll back in my chair. The view on the monitor cuts from the diner to the street as Bron heads for the motel. The techs are bored and yawning, ready for the end of their shift.

I have to admit, giving Bron a physical job was pretty smart. It wears him out early. And once he's in his room, away from everybody, I get some time to think.

This write-me-a-life stuff is not easy. I'm basically making it up as I go. In every writing class, they tell you to start with an outline—work things out in advance, so you won't be surprised. But the truth is, I've never had the patience. And I kind of like being surprised. So I just wing it. Which drives Daisy nuts. On the other hand, watching her and the minions scramble is half the fun.

I pop two beers and walk outside. Once I close the

door behind me, the only light comes from the moon — and from Daisy's laptop screen. There she is, about twenty yards out from the hangar in a lawn chair, just clicking away. I pick up another chair, carry it out and plunk it down next to hers. I hand her one of the beers.

By coincidence we're each wearing a baseball cap with an *S* on it. Only mine is from Salem State — and hers is from Stanford.

I guess she's just going to keep tapping away at her keyboard unless I say something. So here goes...

Chapter 16

ENLIGHTEN ME," I say. "Ten miles away there's a town that's stuck in the Middle Ages. And out here, you've got perfect reception."

She doesn't even look up. "Do you really want me to explain it to you?"

I think for a second. Actually, I don't.

I pull a pack of Marlboros out of my jacket. I take one out and light up.

I'm expecting a lecture from Daisy about damaging the ozone layer. Instead she gets a look like I've never seen on her before. She's staring at me — actually, at the cigarette. I raise my eyebrows. She raises hers.

I hold the pack out. She takes a cigarette and puts it between her lips. She leans over and places the tip of her cigarette against the burning end of mine until hers catches.

She sits back, takes her first deep drag, and closes her eyes.

"Oh, my God," she says. "That is heaven."

Holy shit. A chink in the armor. I decide to push my luck. I want to know more about my main character.

"So Bron has never had a girlfriend?"

Daisy sips her beer and flicks the ash off the tip of her Marlboro. She looks right at me.

"Don't you do any research?"

I admit I'm not exactly Woodward or Bernstein. I write fiction. I make stuff up. And web searches are not a go-to technique for me — especially because I don't own a computer.

"Humor me," I say.

"You want me to start at the beginning?" she asks.

"I do."

I settle back. The slight beer buzz feels great with the cool night air. The only thing missing is a campfire. Because I'm about to hear a story.

First, Daisy tells me, Bron is not one of those up-from-nothing guys. He was born rich. Super rich. Family estate on Boston's North Shore. Summer home on the Vineyard, right next to Carly Simon. Bron was an only child. Dad was an international banker, never home. Mom spent all her time at charity events and sailing. Bron was always kind of a nerdy kid. Loved mechanical stuff and electronics, hated sports. Dad dropped dead during a golf game with Gerald Ford. Mom drowned a year later during a regatta off Nantucket.

Bron skipped his last year of high school. Got a free ride to MIT. Dropped out his sophomore year when he invented a software program to control satellite telemetry.

Time out. "Satellite telemetry?"

"Automated digital communications. The way satellites talk to the controllers and to other satellites. His programs were pure genius. Revolutionary. Everybody wanted them. Business. Government. Military. So he started his own company. Age twenty-two. Then started building and launching satellites of his own. And that's all he's ever done."

"No friends?"

"Maybe a couple work colleagues over the years. But nobody close. He never wanted to mix work with pleasure."

"No problem when all you do is work."

"Bingo."

"No girlfriends? No hot affairs with female astronauts?"

"Has he been on dates? Probably. Here and there. I don't think he's a virgin. But he doesn't really know how to talk to women. Obviously."

Now that I'm on a roll, there's another question I just have to ask.

"So, Daisy…why me? Why do you think somebody with an off-the-charts IQ is reading my books? Why would he pick me for this project instead of some wonk with a Nobel Prize? I don't get it. You're looking at a guy who flunked high school biology."

She takes a slow sip of her beer. "I guess there's no accounting for taste."

True enough.

Daisy and I clink bottles and just sit there side by side, staring at the sky. Out of the corner of my eye, I see her brush a loose strand of hair back from her face and tuck it under her cap.

I have to say, the moonlight looks good on her.

Chapter 17

Two nights later

Knock, knock!

The second he opens the door, Bron feels underdressed. Luke and Timo are waiting on the deck in snug-fit Diesel jeans and matching linen shirts. Timo's buttons are open to expose more of the angel tat than usual. Luke has buffed his bald dome to a high-gloss shine.

"Ready to party?" asks Timo.

"Ready and willing," says Bron. And he means it. Whatever Luke and Timo have in mind is better than another night in his room flipping between channels 9, 11, and 13. Bron pulls the door shut behind him and steps out into the warm night air.

The three of them head off down the street, nodding and waving to people along the way, calling everybody by name. Another novelty for Bron. At his office, he's always running into people he feels he should know, but doesn't. Awkward. Especially because everybody recognizes him. Usually, "Hey, there!" is the best he can do. His workers seem generic, interchangeable. They come and go. But here...he doesn't know how to explain it...everybody stands out in clear focus. Memorable characters.

It's just a three-minute walk to the bar. Bron has passed this place a dozen times, but it always seemed like a place for hardcore locals only. By noon every day there were already a few regulars at their usual spots. At five, they were still there.

But tonight the vibe is totally different. The front of the place is just about empty. Bron, Timo, and Luke head down a narrow pathway between the bar and the tables. There's music coming from the back, and with each step, it gets louder and louder. Somebody in this town knows how to set up a sound system.

They push through a doorway covered by what looks like a flowered living room curtain. Beyond it—the room is packed with people and jumping with energy.

And whoever decked out the town in Christmas lights took it up a notch in here.

The place is glowing.

There's no real bar back here—just a long folding table for the booze and a few industrial-size plastic coolers for beer. But, for this crowd, it's the undisputed center of the universe. And the mood is contagious.

Timo and Luke greet everybody with big smiles, hugs, and backslaps. They may be new in town, but they own the room. Timo pulls out his iPhone and tosses it to the bartender. The bartender patches it into the audio system and flips a switch. Suddenly, the generic club music is replaced by Timo's smartly paced playlist — Pitbull, Bruno Mars, Madonna — and the energy level shoots up even higher.

The man can throw down a mix.

After a couple quick beers, Luke and Timo hit the dance floor — and it's game on.

These guys can move. Really move. The crowd clears some space on the floor as the two of them strut, gyrate, boogie, and bump their way through a thumping Adele track. They're totally into each other — but they also play to the room. By the last measure, their shirts are plastered to their torsos with sweat.

On the downbeat of a Tito Puente salsa track, Timo thrusts his arm out and points into the crowd. He catches the eye of Maria the bank teller. She puts down her drink and moves onto the floor — blushing, but game. Timo can dance rings around her, but he pares his moves down to her level. She's embarrassed and thrilled at the same time. All around them, the dance floor fills with gyrating bodies.

Working her way in from the side, in tight jeans and a halter top, Willow the librarian is showing off some moves that would not be appropriate for story time. Hands weaving in the hair, hips pumping, eyes closed, totally lost in the beat. Now Luke is behind her, hands on her waist, moving right along with her. Crazy. Funny. Steamy.

Bron leans awkwardly against the bar table, sipping a Corona and just trying to stay out of the way. For him, this is strictly a spectator sport. At the opposite corner of the room, thirsty guests are dipping into a beer cooler. Out of the corner of his eye, Bron sees the lid close to reveal a headful of wild blond hair.

Sunny.

No surprise that Bron has never been a big party guy. On the night of his high school prom, he was away at the Westinghouse Science Talent Search. At company gatherings, he always ducks out before the real fun starts. So this might officially be a first for him — seeing a girl across a dance floor and feeling like his heart is about to explode.

Sunny doesn't see him. As she turns, a muscular young man in overalls pulls her onto the dance floor. He swings her, spins her, dips her. And she's no slouch, either — matching him move for move while holding a cold beer in one hand. Bron feels flushed — and it's not from the heat.

He loses sight of Sunny and the stud in the crowd. As he turns to toss away his empty beer bottle, he feels a tap on his shoulder. He turns back. It's Willow — smiling, swaying to the music — and crooking her index finger at him.

No escape.

Out on the floor, Bron's moves are a little stiff — and that's being kind. But Luke takes mercy, coaching him in a few moves that have Willow spinning and laughing in delight as the music gets even louder. She twines her arms around Bron's neck. The sound system blares "Shut Up and Dance." Willow shakes her hair—along with everything else.

Chapter 18

Many hours later

The dance mix fades out and somebody cranks up the Karaoke machine. By now almost everybody in the place is drained and drenched, guzzling beer to replace lost fluids. But some people are still full of energy. Luke is first up on the platform for an impressive rendition of "Say My Name," complete with authentic Beyoncé hair tosses—minus the hair.

The bartender gets bold and decides to shoot for stardom. He gets four bars into "I Love Rock 'n' Roll" before the crowd boos him back to the bar table.

Sunny and Maria are in a corner, heads leaned together over their drinks.

Bron starts to edge his way through the crowd in their direction. Suddenly, he feels a pair of firm hands on his shoulders pushing him toward the stage.

Timo. Strong guy. Resistance is futile.

Now Bron is standing on a beer-soaked square of indoor–outdoor carpeting, holding a sweaty microphone.

Luke and Timo are on either side of him, their beery breath mixing with his.

The tune blasting from the speakers sounds familiar, but the lyrics scrolling across the monitor are all in Spanish. The three Anglos do their best, but they're hopeless.

Fortunately, the room has their back. Half the crowd sings along in Spanish, the other half in English — all at the top of their very drunk voices — beautifully butchering a One Direction classic:

> *I drive all night*
> *To keep her warm*
> *And time is frozen …*

Tyler sees Sunny singing along in a far corner. At least he thinks he does — the Karaoke spotlight is hitting him right between the eyes. And by the time the song ends and he gets a clear view of the room … she's gone.

Chapter 19

Meanwhile, back at the hangar

The techs are already in their bunks, sleeping off a long day. It's just me and Daisy in front of the big flat screen — watching the action wind down.

"That was fun," says Daisy.

Okay. I cock my head, waiting for the other shoe to drop. I know she's not big on compliments, and this one doesn't feel a hundred percent. I feel a *but* coming, and sure enough...

"But you can go deeper," she says. "I think there's more to him."

I admit it. I'm frustrated. I'm tired. It's late. I just created a scenario that felt more complicated than *Gone with the Wind,* and we actually pulled it off. What more does she want from me?

"Look," I say, "I've already uprooted this guy from his normal existence — taken him away from everything he's ever known. Given him new friends, new job. And look at him! Look how he was tonight! He's a totally different guy. All things considered, I think his new life is going pretty well." I'm worked up now. A little pissed off. "What the hell do you mean by *deeper?*"

On the monitor, Bron is walking out of the club, leaning heavily on Luke and Timo—but, to be honest, it's hard to tell who's supporting whom.

"What are we talking about?" I ask. "Cattle stampedes? Tornadoes? Blood orgies? Is that what you want? I'm full of ideas. But I'm not sure you could keep up."

Daisy won't take the bait. She clicks off the monitor and brushes past me on her way to her sleep cubicle, giving me a polite little pat on the shoulder as she goes.

"Think about it, Shakespeare. You'll figure something out."

Just what I need. Another damn editor.

Chapter 20

BRON IS at his usual table at the diner. After a week, he's a regular, along with everybody else in town.

Sunny has settled nicely into her job. So far, she's mixed up only two orders tonight—and Bron's dinner actually arrived hot, with the correct side dish and complete with beverage. Progress.

As Bron digs into his cheeseburger deluxe, he notices a somber group crowded into a booth in the far corner. A mix of young men and women—disheveled, hollow-eyed, burned-out. If it weren't for the fact that they were sitting one booth away from the police chief, you'd think they were part of a meth ring.

"Everything okay?" Sunny is doing her routine waitress flyby. Tyler puts down his burger and nods toward the other side of the diner.

"The people in that booth over there."

She looks. "What about them?"

"Who are they—local drug dealers?" He's only half joking. They all look like they're right on the edge.

"Not quite," says Sunny. "Local schoolteachers."

"Wow. Looks like they had a rough day."

"More like a rough year," says Sunny. She rests her hands on Tyler's table and tells what she's overheard.

Seems that the state has done the town a favor by leaving the local school open all these years. But now the pressure is on from DC to boost the school's STEM scores. Hard enough that half the students need help with English. Now they need to be math wizards and science geniuses, too.

"If the students don't do well on their end-of-year evaluations..."

"What happens?" asks Bron.

"The state closes the school, and the kids get bused to a consolidated district — thirty miles away."

"Well, that definitely sucks."

"Sure does," says Sunny. "And even worse — all those unhappy teachers... they'll be after my job."

Chapter 21

Three hours later

Bron is still at his table. He's nursing his second cup of coffee as the customers thin out to a few stragglers... and then to just him.

"Okay," says Sunny. "No more loitering. I need to close up."

Bron looks around. The kitchen is empty. The cashier is gone. Maria waves as she walks out the door, counting her tips. It's just the two of them. Just like he planned.

"Want some help?"

Sunny gives him a look — playfully suspicious.

"Okay...but don't think you're going to be getting any trade secrets."

"Maybe just the coconut cream pie recipe."

"Forget it. We keep that stored in an abandoned missile silo." She pauses for a couple of seconds, then...

"If you're serious about helping, I've got some boxes to move."

"No problem. Lead the way."

Bron slides out of the booth and follows Sunny through the swinging metal doors to the kitchen, which is surprisingly neat. The chef might be a psycho, but he runs a tight ship. The countertops and range hood are scrubbed clean, and every bowl, spoon, and gadget is in its place. Impressive.

The boxes were a late delivery, and the morning shift will go smoother if Sunny gets them squared away before she leaves. Normally the two young dishwashers would hang around to help, but they skipped out early.

Bron stares at the stack of cartons—marked RICE, FLOUR, and TOMATO PASTE. It's a substantial load, sitting smack in the middle of the back passageway. He grabs the top box. *Ooomph!* Twenty pounds, at least.

"You were going to do this yourself?" Bron asks, trying not to grunt. "Where to?"

"Hey. I'm stronger than I look," she says, grabbing a smaller carton. "Follow me."

Sunny kicks open a single swinging door leading to a large storage room. Fluorescent lights. Dehumidifier in the corner. Huge stacks of cans and kitchen supplies. She nods toward an empty stretch of industrial shelving.

"Right over here," she says. One after the other, they deposit their boxes on the lowest shelf and head back for more.

An hour later, the job is just about done. Sunny has the last of the smaller boxes. She holds the door open as Bron edges in with one of the larger ones. Tight fit. She faces the doorframe and presses flat to give him room. Bron turns and fumbles, a little off balance—and for a nanosecond, his groin presses right up against her butt.

"Sorry! Sorry!" he says, quickly squeezing past.

"No harm, no foul," she says, laughing. She has a great laugh.

After the last box is stored, they plop down on kitchen crates to catch their breath. Bron is physically exhausted, but still jacked on caffeine. Maybe the combo loosens his inhibitions. He stares at her chest. Actually, at her name tag.

"I have to ask," he says. She looks back, knowing exactly where his eyes have been. "Is Sunny a real name, or are you in the witness protection program?"

There's that great laugh again. "Nope. It's for real," she says. "And that's not the best part. Go ahead. Ask me my last name."

"Okay..."

"Day."

It takes Bron a second to put it together. "Day? Sunny Day??" Now it's his turn to burst out laughing. "Are you serious?"

"Yep. Sunny Day. My parents said they always wanted me to be optimistic."

This is great. She's sharing. Bron decides to go for broke. "Well, Sunny Day, can I buy you a beer?"

She gives him a half smile and a little sigh. "Thanks, but I'm driving tonight. I'll treat you to a Diet Coke, though."

He's got no more game.

"Deal."

She takes two plastic cups and fills them from the dispenser. Bron gulps down his drink, savoring the cold, satisfying fizz in his throat.

"Believe it or not," he says, "this has been fun." And he means it.

Well, you have a great future as a furniture mover. The words are in her ear, transmitted through a nearly invisible earpiece.

This is where her improv skills pay off, hearing the dialogue, then turning it into a natural delivery in the moment, seamlessly.

"You have a great future as a furniture mover," she says. Flawless.

Tyler feels himself flushing. He blinks, somehow not able to look directly at her as he formulates his next sentence, but Sunny preempts him.

"Well, I'm going to call it a night. Thanks again for the heavy lifting."

Hug and release, says the voice in her ear, *then exit.*

She wraps her arms around Bron's shoulders, gives him a quick squeeze, then steps back before he can even register what happened. She cocks her head toward the rear hallway.

"This way out."

They step out into the cool night air. The service door shuts behind them with a heavy thud. As his eyes adjust to the dark, Bron sees a black Yamaha dirt bike leaning against the stucco wall behind the building.

"Yours?" Bron asks.

"Beats walking," says Sunny. She grabs the handle-bars, then hikes her skirt way up her thigh. She throws her right leg over the saddle, tugs a helmet over her head, and kick-starts the bike.

"Have a great night," she says, raising her voice over the growl and pop of the two-stroke engine. She drops her visor, rolls the throttle forward, and takes off.

Bron watches her go. For a sweet young waitress, she's not at all timid on the bike. She really leans into those curves.

Almost as if she were trained.

Chapter 22

OUT OF all the minions under Daisy's command, I like the kid named Karl best. He's not just a whiz with remote cameras and mainframe maintenance but also knows the proper temperature for a beer cooler. Which is thirty-eight degrees. Or as Karl would say, "three point three Celsius."

On nights when Daisy and Bron both happen to rack out early, like tonight, Karl and I sometimes break out a couple of cold ones.

"Any way we can get the Red Sox game on that thing?" I'm staring at the massive monitor in the middle of the room, which is currently showing the main street of town. Might as well be a still life.

"Nope. It's a closed circuit. I could probably rewire it though — if I wanted to lose my job."

"Can't have that," I say. "I'd have to manage my own beer supply."

We're both quiet for a while, then Karl asks, "So, is this really what you do for a living — just make stuff up?"

I guess that's a fair way to put it.

"Pretty much," I say. "I write books and just hope people read them."

"Are you on any bestseller lists? Got a fan club? Any groupies?"

"Well, I'll be honest with you, if Tyler Bron didn't love my books, we wouldn't be here right now."

Karl looks puzzled. "Tyler Bron?"

"Right. He's read everything I've ever written — such as it is."

Karl sets his beer down and looks straight at me. "You're kidding, right?"

"What do you mean?"

"What I mean is . . . ask anybody who works for him . . . Tyler Bron has never read anything but a textbook in his entire life."

Chapter 23

*I*N HIS wildest dreams, Bron never imagined himself walking a kid to school. First, he's always had a hard time imagining himself with a kid. Second, that's what those big yellow buses are for, right?

But here he is, just as the sun starts to burn off the morning cool, walking alongside Gonzalo toward the low stucco building that houses grades K through twelve. Fewer than a hundred kids in all, with a lot of mixed-grade classes. And from what Bron knows already, a really overstressed faculty.

"So who's your science teacher?" asks Bron. He wonders why the school's science scores are so low. Lack of effort? Lack of interest?

"Mister Vern. He's funny. He's cool. Everybody likes him."

"And what about you, Gonzalo? You like science?"

"Más o menos," says Gonzalo. "It's okay."

"Okay?" Of course, Bron is prejudiced. Science was his favorite subject from day one. Bio, chemistry, physics, astronomy—you name it, he loved it. Astronomy, especially. Never got a grade below ninety-eight, and to this day he disputes those two points.

Gonzalo leads Bron through the school's narrow corridors. Already, the place is packed with kids and bursting with noise. The decibel level is off the charts, and the pitch of the young voices makes the sound even more intense. Bron backs against the wall as two skinny girls in braids whip past him at top speed. Crazy energy.

"Ladies! Please! No running!" a teacher shouts from a classroom doorway. No use. They're long gone.

"That's him. That's Mister Vern," says Gonzalo, picking up the pace.

Bron recognizes Vern from the diner. Late twenties, already balding—with the remaining wisps of hair flying out wildly in every direction. Sallow complexion.

Stooped posture. Tired eyes.

The day hasn't even started, and this guy already looks beat.

Chapter 24

Three hours later

"So, did you learn anything?" asks Vern with a weary smile.

Bron is sitting with the teacher at a round table at the edge of a courtyard behind the school. There's no cafeteria, so the kids are lunching on whatever they brought from home. Vern is chewing on a peanut butter sandwich, his wild hair waving in the breeze. Tyler just finished sitting in on Vern's class—and the truth is, he learned a lot.

"You really love science, I can tell that," Bron says.

Today's lesson was on dinosaurs, and Vern gave it his all—with uninhibited imitations of pterodactyls and theropods, complete with sound effects. The kids went wild, Gonzalo included.

"I do love it," says Vern. "And I love kids. I just wish there was more we could do here."

"For example?"

"Well, for example, computer studies and online

research. If I'm not mistaken, the only computer in town is somewhere in the back of the library."

"It exists," says Bron with a smile. "I've seen it."

"Basically, we're holding the program together with Elmer's glue and Scotch tape," says Vern. He takes another bite of his sandwich. "Are you in the sciences, Tyler?"

"A little bit. Aerospace. Research. Satellite stuff."

"Excellent. Where'd you go to school?"

The exact phrasing of the question allows Bron to give an honest answer. "MIT."

Vern pauses midbite. "Okay. I'm officially impressed."

Bron sees no point in mentioning that he's still forty-eight credits short of a degree.

As the kids finish their lunches, the courtyard echoes with raucous laughter and yelling and the sound of athletic shoes squeaking against the tile pavement. Bron and Vern are at the edge of a wild churn of activity—so hyper it makes Bron's pulse race.

Out of nowhere, a soccer ball flies toward Bron's head. He flinches just as a kid soars past for a midair interception—inches from his noggin.

"Nice save, Gonzalo," says Vern. "Excellent form."

"¡De nada!" shouts Gonzalo, spinning and laughing as he heads back across the courtyard.

"Perfect example right there," says Vern. "Gonzalo is as bright as they come. Wants to learn. Handles anything I throw at him. But at some point, I just run out of ways to keep him interested."

"Gonzalo's great," says Bron. "I like everything about him except his rooster."

"Zapata?" asks Vern, rolling his eyes. "I'm with you there. I'd put that damned thing in a pot."

A bell rings. A few of the other teachers start to wrangle the kids back into the building. Bron and Vern bring up the rear, collecting the stragglers.

"Great talking to you, Tyler," says Vern. "And listen . . . if you ever want to do a guest lecture or something, let me know. We need all the help we can get."

The whole time, Bron's brain has been turning. He's never been comfortable just standing in the front of a room and presenting. Not his style. But he does have one thought. Something really cool—but not easy to pull off.

"Let me ask you a question," he says.

"Sure," says Vern.

"What's the school policy on field trips?"

Chapter 25

Two weeks and a lot of permission slips later

It's an exceptionally starry night, just as Bron promised.

On a small plateau five miles from the school, the entire student population of the town is squirming excitedly in their sleeping bags. The kids are all wide-eyed and looking up—as special guest Tyler Bron outlines the constellations of the Northern Hemisphere. It's an astronomy lesson in the wild, taught by a guy who clearly knows his stuff.

Vern recruited a few of his fellow teachers to chaperone. He even got Franklin Delgado, the school principal, to show up. Delgado wears a perpetually sour expression—the look of a guy who's totally given up on life. But thirty-two years ago this month, he earned his master's degree in astrophysics, with a specialty in quarks. He loves outer space. And though he'd never admit it, he hasn't had this much fun in a long, long time.

Sunny's here, too. After Bron's help in the stockroom, how could she say no?

The kids are wide awake. Some are staring through cardboard tubes that serve as telescopes. But the person who's most pumped is Tyler Bron. The sky is stunning—wide open and endless. Out here, away from the town lights, the stars seem close enough to touch. It's not much of a stretch to say that, right now, Bron is pretty much in heaven.

Once he gets the kids quieted down, he leads off with astronomy's greatest hits: Orion's Belt. The Dog Star. Arcturus.

Then he moves on to Ursa Major. With broad sweeps of his arm, he outlines the figure of a huge bear four hundred trillion miles away, give or take.

"Over there is the head—a star called Omicron. And the star in the tail—way over there—is called Alkaid. See it? Can everybody see it?"

Slowly, following Bron's enthusiastic gestures, the kids start to make out the shape of a massive beast overhead, with thick legs and a snout pointed east. As one group of kids picks out the pattern, they nudge another group—and so forth across the crowd, until everybody *ooohs* and *ahhs* with recognition. Very cool.

Like kids who grow up bored by a view of the Empire State Building, these kids have never really seen the sky as anything special. It's just there. But now it's a huge screen—filled with ancient warriors and fierce animals and mystical creatures. The sky is alive. Way better than a slide show.

Now it's on to some of Bron's personal favorites. Lyra,

the largest musical instrument in the universe. Pegasus, the majestic horse. The heroic Hercules. Cassiopeia, the original beauty queen. He could go on all night...and he practically does.

For the kids, the best part is when Bron challenges them to spot patterns of their own and name some new constellations on the spot. Gonzalo breaks the ice, shouting "Sidewinder!" Then the ideas come thick and fast, ping-ponging across the plateau—"Elephant's Butt!" "Tarantula!" "Snotball!" And the one that gets the biggest laugh of the night: "Mister Vern's Hair!"

Through it all, Sunny is nestled in a blanket, surrounded by a group of giggling middle-school girls. As the girls stare into the sky, Sunny stares at Bron, silhouetted against the galaxy, with a hundred kids in the palm of his hand.

He is now officially her favorite customer.

Chapter 26

Many hours later

"They look like pod people," Sunny whispers.

She and Bron are making one final patrol through the camp of sleeping kids. The night is getting cold and most are tucked with their heads inside their sleeping bags, grouped in pairs and clusters stretching over a quarter acre. It's a slumber party on an epic scale.

"I've never seen this many kids so quiet," Bron whispers back. "I guess I really know how to put people to sleep."

Sunny punches his shoulder.

"Don't be stupid. They loved every minute of it. And you better watch out—I think a few of the eighth-grade girls have a thing for you."

Beyond the fringe of the crowd, behind a small outcrop of rocks, Bron spreads out the sheet he borrowed from his hotel room. Sunny lays down her own blanket for an extra layer of cushioning. They lie on their backs, side by side, with a few inches between them.

217

Bron finds himself wondering if this girl is too good to be real. But he buries the thought, like he always does. His heart is pounding just to be this close to her. He feels like a school kid himself.

"How did you learn all that...about the sky and the stars?" asks Sunny. "How do you remember all the names?"

Bron gets a quick flashback from his childhood—a pleasant one for a change.

"When I was a kid," he says, "we lived near the ocean. On summer nights, I used to sneak out by myself and just lie on the beach for hours, looking up, memorizing patterns. I remember thinking that in some ways I'd rather be up there than down here."

Sunny tilts her head back to take in the entire expanse overhead. "This is pretty incredible. Where I'm from, I hardly saw any stars at all. Just streetlights and store signs."

"You mean you're not a local?" Bron asks.

Sunny laughs. "Not even close."

She's resting on her elbow now, propped onto her side. Her face is right next to his. She can see that he's tired, finally coming down from the high of the show. He puts his hands behind his head and closes his eyes. He's perfectly still, except for his chest rising and falling. She leans toward him slowly, deliberately, until her lips are almost on his.

"Mr. Bron! I really gotta pee!" A high-pitched call from a few pods away.

Bron and Sunny lurch up to sitting positions. Bron rolls over onto his knees, struggles to his feet and heads off for bathroom duty. He's so groggy that he's not sure what just happened — or almost happened.

But Sunny knows.

Chapter 27

Ssssssssssssssssssss!

The feed is messed up. The monitors are pure snow and the speakers are crackling with static.

It happens at least once a week, but this time for some reason, Daisy has had enough.

She wheels around and shouts at Karl—who happens to be at the console closest to her. "Get the glitch out of this bitch!"

Karl pops out of his chair and heads for the bank of seven-foot-tall IBM mainframes, where the problem usually starts.

I admit I'm always a little amused when Daisy loses her cool. Sometimes I even egg her on just for the fun of it.

But this time, something stops me.

Get the glitch out of this bitch. It's an unusual expression.

I should know—I wrote it. In my first novel.

Which almost nobody read.

Chapter 28

FIRST THING tomorrow, I need you to look at the Durango out front. Something with the computer. Right up your damn alley." It's quitting time for Pico. Bron is wiping the grease off a set of wrenches.

"Will do," says Bron.

Pico's a great boss, but the shop is not really big enough for two people, especially when one of them weighs about three hundred pounds. Bron prefers the times when Pico is in his office sorting through invoices—or when he takes off early, like tonight.

Especially tonight. Because Bron has plans.

As soon as he sees Pico's taillights fade, he starts gathering what he needs.

From a bin of discarded parts, he picks out some thin pieces of sheet metal and plastic pipes, some rubber tubing, and scraps of insulation. A rusting metal cabinet in the back of the shop contains a few decades' worth of discarded chemicals of all kinds, organized in a way only Pico could explain. Just about every element in the periodic table is in there somehow. Bron finds a half-empty box of stump remover, some random solvents, and a few ancient steel wool pads. Perfect.

He packs his treasures into a cardboard box and hoists it onto his shoulder for the walk back to the motel. He was hoping Luke and Timo wouldn't be out on the deck tonight. But no such luck.

They spot Bron and hear the rattle of metal in his box as he tries to slip past.

Caught.

"Hey! What are you making there, Einstein—your own margarita machine?" says Luke.

Bron is too tired to explain. "Nope," he says. "A vibrating bed."

"Smartass," says Timo, grinning.

Luke and Timo look at each other, still curious. But not curious enough to stop drinking. Bron gets a pass.

"Night, guys," he calls out.

Bron closes the door, lowers the shades, and tucks the box into the closet. He realizes that the contents of his cardboard carton are almost enough to put him on a no-fly list.

And he's about to carry them into a classroom.

Chapter 29

*O*NCE UPON *a Starry Night.* This is one of my favorites. It's the best! You'll love it!"

Willow is signing out a picture book at the library. She stamps the card and slips it back inside the jacket, then hands the book to the eager five-year-old boy standing on tiptoes in front of the desk.

The boy's mother tells him to say thank you, but all he can manage is a quick nod. He grips the book to his chest like a priceless treasure. As they walk out, Tyler Bron is on his way in.

"Hey, Willow," says Bron.

"Hey," she answers brightly, then turns mock serious. "I've got a bone to pick with you."

Bron has no idea what she's talking about.

"Thanks to you, we're totally out of books on constellations. Gone. Finito. The shelf is empty."

In the week since Bron's open-air astronomy lesson, the town has been buzzing—especially the kids. Bron had never been asked for his autograph before. But now it's happened a few times.

"Sounds like I'm good for business," says Bron.

"So, what's up?" Willow strokes her fingers through her hair and cocks her head to one side. "You need the computer again?" She bores her eyes into his. "Need to delve deeper into your life?"

"Actually," says Bron, fiddling with some pencils on the checkout desk, "I need to take it with me."

Willow stops playing with her hair. "The computer? What do you mean—*take it with you?*"

"I'm helping with a science project at the school. It involves digital control. And you've got the only programmable hard drive in town."

Willow thinks this over.

"I'll get it back, right?"

"Absolutely."

"In working order?"

"Probably."

Willow leans forward. "Oh, What the hell. Go ahead. To be honest, I prefer the card catalog anyway." She leans forward a little more. "I like having something in my hand. Something I can touch..." Crazy flirty.

Nice try. Bron is already on his way to the back.

He has to crawl on all fours underneath the study carrel to trace the power cord and modem cord to the outlets. He encounters about twenty years of dust and a box of petrified Gummy Bears.

When he backs out and stands up again—surprise— Willow is right there, leaning with her back against the wall just a few feet away. Bron could swear that her blouse is opened at least one button lower than it was before.

"So, Fred Astaire, when are we going dancing again?" she asks.

Bron tugs the power cord through the opening in the desktop and starts wrapping it around the computer.

"Are we allowed to discuss dancing during library hours?"

"I don't see any rules posted," she says, moving toward him.

"Sorry I'm late!" Sunny barges around the corner, out of breath. "I just finished my shift—"

Willow halts in midstep, eyebrows raised.

"No problem," says Bron, "I just got this thing disconnected. If you can carry the CPU, I can get the monitor. Willow, you know Sunny, right?"

Willow smiles, kind of.

"Not sure," she says. "Oh, wait…I remember…you're Sunny…the waitress." Bit of an edge there, but Sunny lets it go.

"Yep. That's me. Sunny the waitress. Everything good?"

"Never better," says Willow.

If Bron weren't so preoccupied with detaching the cable between the CPU and the back of the monitor, he might pick up on the tension in the air. But he gets nothing. He lifts the base unit and hands it to Sunny. He grabs the monitor and balances the keyboard on top, cables dangling everywhere.

"Thanks, Willow," says Bron.

"We really appreciate this," says Sunny.

"Namaste," she says. "Just don't break it."

"We'll be careful, I promise," says Bron.

On the way out of the back hall, Bron catches a glimpse of a metal periodical rack. There, on the bottom shelf, is an issue of *Scientific American* from 2001. Tyler recognizes the face on the cover. It's his. Different time. Different guy.

Outside, Sunny pauses to get a better grip on the computer. "Be honest," she says, "what's the worst that could happen with this thing?"

"A computer this old?" says Bron. "It could blow up."

Willow watches them leave, then hangs the WE'LL BE BACK AT... sign in the door. She swings the clock hands on the sign to an hour from now. It's been a busy morning, and she's all out of goddamn star books, anyway.

Walking toward the back hallway, she reaches into her purse and pulls out a joint.

A big, fat one.

Chapter 30

"NICELY DONE," says Daisy, and I have to agree.

Sometimes I surprise myself with the way the words on the page end up on the screen. Sunny's timing was impeccable.

Daisy and I are sitting together on the sofa in the back of the control room. Because we're both in such a positive mood, I decide to see if I can peel a few more layers from Ms. DeForest.

"So, you met Bron when?" I ask it as if she's told me before. Which she hasn't. She gives me a look.

"I interned for him," she says, "when I was still in law school."

"A Ph.D. intern?"

"Look. Everybody at the company was overqualified. We just wanted to be part of it. Bron was doing things that had never been done. It was exciting."

"So what were your duties?" I ask. "Bringing him pizza?"

"I worked on clearing patents. I'm not sure he even knew who I was." She shakes her head. "Thinking back, I'm not sure he knew who anybody was."

"So how did you get from there to here?"

I consider myself a keen observer of body language. And I've noticed that whenever Daisy doesn't want to answer a question, she does a quick nose-crinkle — like a kid refusing broccoli.

"I don't know," she says. "I moved into operations and logistics. I guess he thought I had the right skill set."

"So you hatched this scheme together — the two of you?"

Daisy scoots herself off the sofa — nose-crinkling big-time.

"Okay, Shakespeare, that's it. Back to your Smith Corona."

"It's a Selectric."

Chapter 31

ID YOU bring the powdered sugar?" asks Bron. He holds out his palm like a surgeon waiting for a scalpel.

Sunny reaches into her bag and hands him a five-pound bag of confectioners' superfine, packed so tight it feels like a brick.

"Perfect." Bron adds it to the pile of ingredients and parts on the worktable.

Bron and Sunny are in Vern's classroom, surrounded by a delegation of kids from every grade. A group of teachers looks on from behind. Principal Delgado's face is pressed up against the small square window in the door.

A tiny third-grader pipes up. "Are we making cookies?"

"Absolutely not," says Bron. "What we're mixing would, well . . . it would make your tummies explode."

The kids laugh. But he's not joking.

Sunny sits down at one of the classroom desks, lowering the top across her lap and folding her hands politely, as if she were back in Catholic school. Or acting class.

Vern pulls up a desk next to her.

"I should have taken the day off," he says in a stage whisper. "Nothing to do but watch the maestro at work."

He's right. Bron is terrific with the kids—totally in control. He's laser focused on the task, and they're right there with him. Over the past week, they've sorted and measured the parts and made a construction diagram on graph paper. Now, with the kids' help, Bron clips, slides, and glues bits of metal and plastic together until a shape begins to form on the worktable. The buzz in the room picks up. Teachers nod. Kids point. The little ones start to bounce on their toes, angling for a better look.

And suddenly, there it is: A thin, upright cylinder about four feet tall. Some rudimentary fins. The beginnings of a nose cone. Crude. Ghetto-rigged. MacGyvered. Say what you want. But it's clearly and unmistakably... a rocket. And a pretty cool-looking one at that.

As he tinkers, Bron explains what he's doing. He spills out information so fast that some of the younger students have a hard time following, especially if they're new to English.

Thrust. Pitch. Roll. Attitude. *¿De qué está hablando?* What the heck is he talking about?

Gonzalo leans down to translate for his smaller schoolmates until he sees their eyes light up—just like his.

The truth is, Gonzalo feels lucky—and a little proud of himself. After all, he was the one who spotted this pasty gringo wandering in the desert. And now, thanks to him, his school is going to have the most kick-ass science project of all time.

Chapter 32

DAISY IS amazing. And so are her nerds.

I don't know how the hell they got cameras into that classroom. Maybe they tapped into the school security system. Or maybe they invented some kind of miniature lens that looks like a fly on the wall. I've stopped asking questions, but I wouldn't put it past them.

Right now, Daisy is sitting across from me with her feet up, her nose buried in her laptop. Even after all this time, she still feels like she needs to babysit me. But honestly, I don't mind the company.

I'm pecking away at my Selectric, working out ideas for tomorrow. It feels like everything is finally flowing. A well-oiled machine. Maybe I don't suck at this after all.

Out of nowhere, the metal outer door opens and slams.

"I am *done!* Can you hear me? *DONE!*"

I know that voice.

Daisy sits bolt upright as a woman walks into the control room. It's Sunny.

I definitely did *not* write this. Sunny is still in her

waitress outfit. Her eyes are red. It's the first time she's set foot in this place since her audition.

"Wait! Hold on! What's the matter?" says Daisy, rushing over to put her hand on Sunny's shoulder. Sunny pulls away—not having any of it.

"I can't do it. I can't do this anymore."

She's not crazed. She's not yelling. She's just... determined.

This situation is way out of Daisy's wheelhouse. Mine, too. But I give it a try.

"What do you mean?" I say. "It's working really well! He's crazy about you!"

Sunny takes a step forward and jabs her finger at me.

"Working? Sure. Because you're making it work. You talk me through every step. You give me all the questions and all the answers—you and your—" She points at my typewriter.

"It's a Selectric."

"And all this...this *Mission: Impossible* bullshit!" She waves her arm around at our multimillion-dollar lair— consoles, monitors, mainframes. "This has nothing to do with the real world!"

The minions are stunned. They just sit there.

Daisy decides to switch up her approach.

"Wait now. Wait a minute. You knew what you were signing up for. This isn't some dorky school play you can quit if you don't like your part. You need to see this through. You're committed—like all of us. You signed an agreement."

"That's pathetic," says Sunny. "You can keep your stupid money. And don't worry, I won't run and sell my story to the *Enquirer*. I know what I signed. I'm just sick and tired of being a fake. I don't know if you can tell from inside your little cocoon here—but Tyler Bron is a good guy. He's a really good guy. He deserves something better than a grade C actress."

For a second I think about telling Sunny what a terrific actress she's turned out to be, but I don't think it would go over too well right now.

Sunny turns to walk out—and then turns back. She tugs her hair away from her right ear, then prods with her little finger until a tiny receiver pops out into her hand. She tosses it onto a desktop.

"I know you'll want that back," she says. "I'm sure it's really expensive."

And she's gone.

Daisy stands there for a few seconds. Then she walks slowly across the room and sits down on the sofa. She looks at me.

"Oh. Shit," she says. "This is big trouble."

Like I don't know it. A huge part of Bron's life just walked out the door. A huge part of my life. If this doesn't get fixed, the whole project collapses. Right on top of me.

I hate to sound selfish at a time like this, but without Sunny, I've got no ending.

Chapter 33

BRON WRAPS up his last oil change of the day and makes it to the diner by eight, just like clockwork. He takes his usual seat and settles in to watch the crowd. Way more interesting than TV. When he feels Sunny at his elbow, he looks up and smiles at...

Maria?

"Hi, there," he says, trying to cover his disappointment. "I'm sorry. Where's Sunny tonight?"

Maria fiddles with her order pad and pen.

"She didn't say anything to you?"

"Say what? Where is she?"

Maria takes a short breath and lets it out. "She's gone."

Bron gets a stabbing pang in his gut. "What do you mean, *gone?*"

"Quit. Left. Walked out last night."

Bron thinks back twenty-four hours. He was working late at the school. He and Vern split a microwave pizza in the break room. Then he went right back to the motel.

"Wait," says Bron, "I don't understand. She just...left? Without saying anything?" Now his heart is pounding.

"She looked upset. Said she didn't have time to explain. She picked up her tips and her paycheck and split."

At this point, Bron is practically jumping out of his skin. His mind is spinning. What's going on? Did he say something? Did he not say something? Did something happen? Why would she just take off like that? In one swift move, he slides out of the booth. Maria backs up to avoid getting bowled over.

"Where does she live? *Where does she live?*" Bron is almost out the door already and has to stop to catch Maria's answer.

"About five miles outside of town — Alba Road. I think she was just renting. Let me know if you find out anything —"

Bron doesn't hear a word after "Alba Road."

With all this frantic energy, he could probably run the five miles in about fifteen minutes. That's nuts. He needs directions. He needs a ride. The street is empty. Hold on. He sees headlight beams.

A pickup truck is coming slowly around a corner the next street down. Bron starts jogging and waving his arms.

He knows that truck. He knows that driver.

Chapter 34

GRANDPA'S EYES aren't what they used to be, so after dark, he takes it slow. But that's okay with Bron. Gives him time to scan the shoulder of the road as they go. But for what? Footprints? Blood? Breadcrumbs?

After about ten minutes, the truck headlights bounce off a battered sign marking Alba Road. Not far from the intersection is a small stucco bungalow—the only building for a hundred yards. This has to be it.

Grandpa pulls to a stop. "¿*Debería esperar?* Should I wait, Señor Tyler?"

"No. I don't want her to think I brought a posse. I'm good."

As Grandpa makes a swerving U-turn, Bron walks across the sand and low scrub grass to the house. The porch light is on, but everything else is dark. He knocks on the front door. Nothing.

He walks quickly around the house, pressing his face against the windows, one by one. No sounds. No movement.

Back at the front door, Bron tries the knob. Locked.

He looks under the mat and in a clay planter. No key. Just as he's about to put his elbow through a window, he notices a magnetic sticker on the metal mailbox. It's from Verde Repairs. NO JOB TOO SMALL it says — in English and in Spanish. Bron peels it off.

He slips the thin sticker in against the strike plate of the doorjamb and wiggles it until he feels a slight give. Old school, but it works. He's in. He flips the light switch just inside the door.

"Sunny? It's Tyler. You here?"

He moves quickly through the living room, kitchen, and bedroom, flicking lights on as he goes. Deserted.

The rooms are bare except for some IKEA-style furniture. The bed is made — not perfect, but neat. No signs of a struggle, as they say on the cop shows. He slides the bedroom closet door open. Empty — except for one white blouse and one black skirt.

He checks the medicine cabinet. Contact lens solution, toothpaste, aspirin — the usual. Not much in the refrigerator — just a carton of orange juice, some cottage cheese, and a couple of beers.

Bron pulls open the kitchen drawers and finds some plastic flatware and paper napkins.

And then...he feels something. Something that doesn't quite fit. Tucked under a cheese grater and a pair of oven mitts is an eight by ten manila envelope, the kind with a metal clasp at the top.

Bron opens the clasp. Pulls out the contents. And feels his heart thud through his chest.

Chapter 35

*H*E'S LOOKING at a stack of identical black-and-white glossy photos. They're headshots — the standard calling card for models and actors. A dozen copies.

The name printed in script at the bottom of the photo is "Sunny Lynn Aberday."

His stomach freezes.

Of course it's her, but somehow not her. The hair is shorter and straighter, with some serious studio styling — and her freckles are missing. Photoshopped clean off. To the right of the full-face photo are two smaller head-to-toe shots in color — one showing her in a red bikini, the other in a flower-print sundress. Girl-next-door gorgeous. On the back are her vital stats: hair color, eye color, height, weight, measurements. The rest of the résumé is brief.

She studied theater at Buffalo State. Took a few acting classes in New York. She was "Juror #4" in an episode of *Law & Order,* "Earth Human" in the finale of *Battlestar Galactica,* and "Zumba Girl" in a sit-com pilot called *Atlantic Motion.*

Special Skills: Horseback riding, skiing, motorcycles.

Bron feels a burning adrenaline rush that starts in his chest and courses down his arms. He whips the pile of photos against the wall with everything he's got. The headshots scatter and flutter to the floor. For a few moments, the room is raining Sunny.

Bron is furious. With her. With himself. His mind spins back through every interaction, every conversation. How easily he got led along. But was he any better? After all, he asked Crane to write him a life. He just didn't know how it would feel to lose it.

He shoves the back door open and kicks over two empty garbage cans. As he turns back toward the house, he catches a glint of chrome. Tucked into a corner next to some garden tools is a Yamaha dirt bike, key still in the ignition.

Bron hasn't ridden anything with two wheels since he was sixteen. He hops onto the saddle and turns the key. No juice. He puts his foot on the starter pedal and shoves down hard. The engine sputters, then dies. He tries again. This time it fires up.

He gives the bike some gas and takes off, nearly knocking over a rain barrel as he swings around the house and swerves onto the road, heading farther away from town — out into the empty desert.

He's really cranking now. He squints his eyes and clenches his mouth tight as all kinds of airborne critters collide with his face. The road is pitch black, except for the bouncing white arc of his headlight beam.

He doesn't know where he's going—just knows that he has to keep moving and looking for answers. Looking for her. Forty miles per hour on the speedometer. Then fifty...

His head is buzzing with a thousand thoughts. Suddenly, he sees—

BAM!

Chapter 36

*I*T HAPPENS in the blink of an eye. And I'm watching it in HD.

Daisy screams.

Bron's bike jolts to the side and flips. For a second everything is a blur—then totally still.

Now the night-vision sensors are picking up two heat signatures about twenty feet from the road. One is the bike engine. The other is Bron. Neither is moving.

A few of the minions jump up from their stations.

"Stop!" Daisy yells. "Stay right where you are!"

She looks at me and grabs a set of keys off a table. "Let's go!"

We run out the back and hop into a Jeep. Daisy gets behind the wheel—as if I had a choice.

Before I can buckle my seat belt, she spins the Jeep around. I almost fly out the side. We bounce like crazy over ruts and rocks all the way to the main road. As soon as Daisy feels pavement under the tires, she floors it.

The techs back at the hangar are feeding directions into her Bluetooth as we go—but it's not like there are a lot of roads out here to choose from. We make two turns and then it's a straight shot to the scene. She counts down the distance as we approach: "One mile... half mile... two hundred yards!"

She brakes hard and yanks the Jeep onto the shoulder. In the middle of the road, just in front of Bron's skid marks, is a crushed armadillo. Gross.

Daisy slams the shift lever into park and jumps out. She gets to Bron in about two seconds. I click the high beams to light them up. Bron is moving! He sits up slowly and Daisy grabs his arm. She helps him to his feet. In the headlight beams, I can see a patch of blood on his forehead. His shirt is shredded. But he's walking and talking. He's in one piece. The sand dune behind him must have made one hell of an airbag.

Chapter 37

WEIRD. I'M flashing back to my first meeting with Daisy—the one where she laid down the rules.

Rule number one: No contact with Tyler Bron.

Consider that rule busted.

"Are you okay?" I ask. "Anything broken?"

"I'm fine," Bron says evenly. He shakes off Daisy's help.

"Where the hell were you going?" she asks.

"What?" he says coldly. "You mean it's not in your mission plan?"

All of a sudden he's right up in my face—madder than I've ever seen anybody. But controlled. Really, tightly controlled.

"She really sucked me in. And you were just stringing me along...like some kind of puppet!"

"You should sit down," says Daisy. "Take it easy for a minute."

But he's not done. I take a step back. I'm worried that he's going to uncork a punch. But he stays at a low burn, which almost makes it worse.

"You know, I had a life. And it wasn't a terrible life.

And maybe I shouldn't have been so quick to change it. It's my fault. I can see it now for what it was. At least I knew what was real and what wasn't. This was all a big mistake."

He looks straight at me and points. "Starting with you."

Before I can say anything, he hops in the Jeep. He puts it into gear and takes off—back the way he was heading. Somewhere in the general direction of civilization.

Daisy and I are standing in the middle of the road like idiots. That's when I lose it.

"DAMN IT!"

I'm shouting at myself, at Daisy, at the whole stinking desert. "I just blew everything. How the hell did this happen? I just threw away my last chance! I *blew* it!"

Daisy is calm—and in no mood for any of my shit.

"Hey. Shakespeare," she says, "this is not about you."

She walks back down the incline to where the Yamaha is lying in the sand. As she pushes it up the slope, I grab the handlebars and tug it the rest of the way onto the shoulder.

Bent fender. Dented exhaust pipe. Cracked headlight lens. It could have been a lot worse.

Daisy swings her leg over the saddle and kick-starts the bike on the first try. She wheels it around and points it back toward the hangar. Bron is long gone.

"Well?" she says. "Don't just stand there. Climb on."

I straddle the seat from the back, inching my way forward, trying my best to give Daisy some room up front. But the seat was not exactly built for two. No matter how

I maneuver, my crotch is crowding her rear end and my knees are pressing up against her thighs. I try gripping the sides of the seat for support as she takes off, but that lasts for about two seconds. My survival instinct takes over and I lock my hands around her middle, my chin pressed against her back. At this point, we're melded into one crazy rolling *Kama Sutra* position.

"Hold tighter," she yells over the engine noise, "I promise I won't press charges."

I clench my hands together and tuck my arms in close, just under her rib cage—the no-man's-land between her belly button and her breasts.

"Is this thing safe?" I shout into her ear.

"Beats walking!" she shouts back.

Where have I heard that before?

Chapter 38

PRINCIPAL DELGADO is looking out his office window when the angels of doom arrive. The plain gray sedan with government plates pulls into a visitor parking spot behind the school.

This is it.

Two State Department of Education administrators emerge from the car, with expressions as sober as their suits. Eric Baynes is the lead—a DOE lifer. Ellie Cabot, the one carrying the thick binder, is a trainee. She's here to observe. To learn the procedure. To see exactly what notifications and documents are required to shut down a school for good.

The minute they walk into the building, there's a disturbance in the hive. By the time Delgado's office door shuts behind them, secretaries are whispering to teachers and teachers are whispering to other teachers— and kids are picking up the vibrations. The rumors are true. The executioners are here.

A few eighth-grade boys volunteer to let the air out of their tires.

But one kid has a better idea . . .

Chapter 39

GONZALO PLANTS himself strategically in an alcove near Delgado's reception area — the area where you sit when you get called to the principal's office. He checks his pocket to make sure everything is ready. He's worked on this for a long time, thinking it through, just waiting for the day to come.

Kids pass back and forth — but with a different energy than usual. A lot of glances toward the office and murmurs behind cupped hands. Only the youngest kids are oblivious, zipping along with overloaded backpacks at their usual Road Runner pace.

Gonzalo has a bead on Delgado's door. When he sees it open, he makes his move. In one glance he sizes up the situation and chooses his target.

"Send those reports along as soon as they're finalized and we'll be in touch."

Baynes is talking to Delgado, who has his tie loosened and his sleeves rolled up.

"No problem," says Delgado, eyes down.

Baynes brushes past Gonzalo, but Ellie Cabot runs right into him. Gonzalo makes sure of it. He connects with her hip, almost causing her to drop her binder. Now she's even more flustered than before. She looks down as Gonzalo stumbles backward, selling it hard.

"Oh, no! I'm so sorry—are you all right?" she says.

Delgado is on his way back into his office. He turns around.

"No problem, Señora," Gonzalo says, recovering nicely, "but since you're here…" He reaches into his pocket and whips out a folded piece of paper—hand-lettered and illustrated.

"I'd like to invite you to our school science demonstration," he says. He thrusts the paper up at her, giving her no choice. She takes it, keeping her other hand tight around the binder.

"Time and coordinates are right there at the bottom."

Baynes turns around to see what's going on. What's this kid doing—trying to sell raffle tickets?

"Cabot—let's go!" says Baynes.

Ellie reads the invitation as she walks. Gonzalo matches her step for step, looking right up into her face.

"Please," he says, "you won't be sorry. It will be spectacular."

She stops. "Thank you…?" She waits for a name.

"Gonzalo. Gonzalo Martino Alvarez."

"Thank you, Gonzalo. I…we…will try. We will." She catches Delgado's eye. He gives her a thin smile.

Ellie tucks the paper into the side pocket of her suit jacket and hurries out the door to catch up with her supervisor.

In his heart, Gonzalo knows he chose his target well. Just from her expression, he can tell that Ellie Cabot is a woman who really, really hates her job.

Chapter 40

*I*F YOU asked Tyler Bron to say what he missed the most about home, it wouldn't be central air-conditioning or fresh fruit or even his boxed set of Carl Sagan's *Cosmos.*

It would be this: He's standing in a construction hangar the size of two football fields. He owns it.

Like everybody else in sight, he's wearing a unisex 3M cleanroom suit.

Scattered around the massive space are huge platforms supporting several works in progress. Technicians swarm over an assortment of gleaming space-bound devices. A chorus of electronic beeps blends with light metallic tapping and the *vvrrip-vvrrip* of precision torque wrenches.

Standing in the center of it all, Bron is looking up at a nearly completed six-ton communications satellite. Parts of the device are still shrouded in protective foil or shrink-wrapped in plastic.

Bron's presence adds a new level of intensity to the

hum. A foreman spots him from the platform and waves him up to survey his latest five-hundred-million-dollar baby.

"Come on aboard! She's just about ready to fly!"

Bron ascends a metal ladder step by step, being careful not to let his white booties slip off the treads.

The satellite is nearly twenty feet long and fifteen across — about half the size of a city bus. Hardened titanium encases miles of delicate wiring and integrated circuitry. Curved surfaces gleam with shiny gold Mylar blanketing. Dark solar panels are folded close to the sides like bat wings.

Bron leans into a hatch on the central module as his foreman waves a Maglite beam around the interior.

"Reaction control?" asks Bron.

"Perfect."

"What about the RF multiplexer?"

The foreman winces slightly. "The whole repeater needs some tweaks."

"How long?"

"Forty-eight hours, tops."

Problems or not, the language feels good to Bron. Cool. Precise. Real.

In fact, for the whole week he's been back, he's been wallowing happily in data streams and digital readouts. He wakes to a hundred business emails a day and taps himself to sleep on his laptop.

He tries not to think about her. And mostly, it's working.

As Bron descends the ladder, he moves past a stout woman on an aluminum scaffold, her eyes focused on a long, curved panel in front of her. Slowly, meticulously, she peels a stencil backing to reveal the final numeral in the satellite's official designation: BRON-14

She looks over as he passes.

"Good to have you back, Mr. Bron."

At the bottom of the ladder, another worker holds out an iPad. Bron ticks a configuration approval with his index finger. As he walks off, the hum behind him returns to something like normal.

Whoosh!

Bron passes through the airlock that separates the construction bay from the main office complex. He unzips his disposable outfit and sits on a stainless-steel bench bolted to a spotless tile floor—so white it's practically blinding.

His mind is humming pleasantly with the tasks ahead of him this afternoon—a meeting with Atlas V engineers, conference calls with bidders for antenna components, and an update with the Space Surveillance Network—to make sure that BRON-14 won't accidentally bump into any of the four thousand other satellites already circling the globe.

Even if he wanted to think about her, he doesn't have time. He's made sure of it.

As he tugs off one of his cotton booties, his loafer

comes with it. Along with the tiniest trickle of desert sand.

Damn it!

He throws the shoe against the wall, where it makes the only black mark in a very, very clean room.

Chapter 41

EVERYTHING MUST go.

The back of the cargo plane looks like a giant open mouth. Daisy's minions are rolling mainframes and consoles out of the hangar and up the ramp. The plane crew is fastening everything tight with thick yellow straps. Lots of sweating. Not much talking.

I'm sitting outside on top of the beer cooler. Karl promised to ship it to my home address, and I want to be sure it doesn't get lost in the shuffle. I need to salvage at least one good thing out of this disaster.

Daisy is supervising the load-out. She's standing with her hands on her hips like General Patton. She knows the location and destination of every cable. I bet the entire inventory is in her head.

She walks over and tucks her Ray-Bans into her hair like a headband.

"Squeeze over," she says, and sits down next to me. She sits there quietly for a while, watching the operation proceed. Then she says, "It's not your fault."

Like hell.

"Sure it is. I'm the writer. I create the world. I control the characters. And I couldn't make it work. Endings are always the hardest part—but I never even got a chance to figure it out."

Daisy is staring out across the runway—actually just a long stretch of sand that happens to be flatter than the rest of the sand around it.

"You worked hard," she says, "and you made him better. You made him a better character than he ever was. Trust me. I know."

A row of minions walks by with monitors and flat screens. Daisy gets up to supervise the loading. She turns back to me.

"You gave him what he needed," she says. "Let him write his own ending."

I can't believe I'm thinking this, but I'm really going to miss Daisy DeForest. She can definitely be a pain in the ass—but as it turns out, she's not a half bad muse.

Chapter 42

ONZALO, YOU do the honors."

In the middle of the classroom, Mr. Vern steadies his star pupil by the belt as he reaches for the very top of the rocket. With his fingers stretched, Gonzalo places a hollow balsa wood nose cone right on the tip.

The rocket is fantastic: slender and smooth, painted in red and gray school colors, with four thick black rubber fins at the bottom. Long connecting wires extend from the base to a crude junction box—and from there to the back of the ancient Dell computer, which sits precariously on a nearby desk.

It may be the first suborbital vehicle in history constructed from a muffler pipe and mud flaps—but it's got a functioning altimeter and radio control. And to the kids in the room, it's just about the coolest thing they've ever seen.

As everybody cheers, Gonzalo looks hopefully toward the door. Where is Tyler Bron? Why isn't he here? It's been a whole week. He just... disappeared.

After the first day Bron didn't show up, Gonzalo got

his *abuelo* to open the door to his room at the motel. Everything was still there, including the shorts and T-shirts Gonzalo found for him. He'd be back. Right? Nobody just walks off in the middle of a project. Not a project this important.

Vern follows Gonzalo's gaze and tries to distract him with a little cheerleading, raising his voice so the whole room can hear.

"Hey. You guys all did a terrific job. This is first-class. Really impressive."

"The telemetry still isn't right," Gonzalo says, climbing down from the chair. He taps a few keys on the computer and brings up a sample pattern. To Vern, it looks like his latest EKG. At this point, the kids know more than he does. And no wonder. They were taught by a master.

"We've got only two days," says Gonzalo. "We need to get this done."

The other kids are right with him. As the younger ones run their fingers over the rocket's smooth fuselage, Gonzalo's classmates and some of the older kids huddle around the computer and break out their calculators and notepads. A mini mission control.

Failure is not an option.

The truth is, Vern and every other teacher in the room has given up on this terrific project's making one whit of difference. They've all got their résumés ready, just marking time until the final bell of the final day.

But Gonzalo hasn't given up. Not by a long shot.

Chapter 43

Two nights later

Showtime.

The whole town is gathered on the plateau—the exact spot where Bron gave his astronomy lecture. But tonight, there's a cloud cover. The sky looks like black velvet.

Vern fires up the generator. The computer comes to life. A mild cheer from the crowd. So far, so good.

A red Mazda Miata rolls slowly across the sandy pathway to the launch site. Luke and Timo high-five everybody from the car windows as they inch toward the front row for the best possible view.

As Vern and a couple of the other teachers secure the launch platform, Gonzalo scans the dark desert.

At first, nothing. Then...two yellowish dots in the distance.

Headlights! It could be him!

Gonzalo runs to the edge of the plateau and watches the vehicle on its climb up the winding dirt road.

The car reaches the top and stops at the far end of the crowd. A gray sedan.

It's not Bron. It's the Department of Education.

The driver's side door opens. Ellie Cabot steps out. Business casual wardrobe tonight. After a few seconds, the passenger side door opens. It's Baynes, her boss. Still wearing a damn suit. At least he left his tie in the car.

Ellie waves. Gonzalo waves back. His invitation worked. But now what? The angels of doom have arrived to witness his science project and pass judgment on the whole school. And his mentor is MIA.

No pressure.

As Vern holds up his hands to quiet the crowd, Gonzalo and his crew review their calculations and procedure one last time. They hardly hear what their teacher is saying in the background...

"Thank you all for coming tonight. We are here to see something truly amazing. A self-propelled rocket designed and built by your children." Beat. "Without much help from me!" Laughs and polite applause.

"Now, I'd like to ask Gonzalo Alvarez and his team to unveil their project."

Gonzalo steps to the launch platform and takes one corner of the drop cloth covering the rocket. He nods to three other kids. They each take hold of one length of the plastic, just like they practiced. On Gonzalo's signal, they yank the cover down to reveal their handiwork—dramatically lit by the headlights on Grandpa's pickup.

There's a huge roar from the crowd. So loud it almost covers the sound coming from the sky—*thunka, thunka, thunka*—getting louder and louder...

A piercing spotlight beam lights up the scene from above. Sand swirls as a sleek helicopter circles and lands on the far edge of the plateau. As the rotors wind down, the lone passenger steps out.

The kids all turn and run toward the chopper like a pack of puppies. But Gonzalo gets there first.

He buries his face in Tyler Bron's chest.

Chapter 44

*F*LIGHT CONTROL, begin the countdown!" Bron stands in the middle of the crowd of kids as all eyes shift to the launch pad.

Gonzalo shouts out as his finger hovers over the designated launch key: *V* for "Vern."

"Ten…Nine…Eight…" and so on…"Three…Two… One! Ignition!

Gonzalo presses the button. Nothing.

A huge groan rises from the crowd. Baynes gives Ellie a sideways "I told you so" glance. Kids bite their lips and put their hands over their faces.

Bron steps forward and wiggles the connections. He taps at a few more keys.

"Hold it!" A woman's voice comes from the crowd.

The front line of spectators parts for Willow. Short skirt. Bare feet. She walks right up to the back of the computer table. She does a quick mental measurement of the computer case…and then whacks it on the left side with her flat hand. Really hard.

The digits on the monitor screen blink twice, then hold steady.

Willow looks at Bron. "Sometimes you just need to hit it over the head."

Bron folds his hands together and gives her a half bow. "Namaste." Wrong use of the word, but she gets the idea. Bron turns back to the kids.

"Flight Control, repeat the countdown."

Gonzalo starts again, his heart pounding. "Ten... Nine..."

At eight, the crowd picks up the cadence and counts along.

At four, Gonzalo looks up at Bron.

Bron says, "Wait. Hold the countdown."

Gonzalo looks up, puzzled. What now? Bron leans over and whispers, "I just need a minute."

Bron pulls a Sharpie marker from his pocket and walks to the launch platform. He leans over and christens the rocket with a name, writing on the fuselage in clear block letters:

SUNNY-1

He turns to Gonzalo and calls out. "Flight Control... proceed!"

Gonzalo yells, "Three... Two... One! He presses the V key. "Ignition!"

Instantly, a stream of red-yellow flame shoots out of

the base of the rocket, along with a belch of gray smoke. The slender cylinder seems to tremble on the platform and then, it doesn't just lift off... it *BLASTS* off!

In one second it's a hundred feet in the air, then two hundred. A stream of smoke marks the path into the sky until it disappears. The computer screen lights up with a tracking arc—a quick upward curve, then a smooth taper downward.

At exactly one minute and thirty seconds into the flight, the screen blinks the words: "Parachute Deployed." A cheer goes up from the kids around the computer. From somewhere in the crowd, a rooster crows with gusto.

Two miles away in the dark desert, a red-and-gray rocket floats gently to the ground. In the morning, it will be retrieved by a bunch of deliriously happy kids. But for now, mission accomplished!

It actually happened! The flight team is thrilled. Bouncing. Hugging. Laughing. It all worked! The fuel. The flight. The tracking. Everything!

Gonzalo looks at Ellie, standing at the edge of the crowd. Ellie looks at Baynes, who stands next to her with his arms folded. Baynes looks over at Delgado—and nods.

Delgado knows what that nod means. It means a reprieve. Not forever. Not for long. But maybe, at least, for another year. Baynes is smart enough to know you don't coldly close down a school this cool. Bad PR.

Gonzalo runs to Ellie, but her body language warns

him that a hug is not appropriate. She's doing her best to maintain her businesslike composure. After all, her boss is right there.

"Well done, young man," says Baynes, extending his hand to Gonzalo. Gonzalo shakes it.

Ellie reaches out to shake Gonzalo's hand, too. Instead, Gonzalo tugs her down by the arm until her face is almost level with his—then kisses her cheek with a loud smack. Ellie covers her face with her hand, hiding a very broad smile.

Alphonse Delgado, school principal and former astrophysics major, wipes something from his eye. Probably just a speck of sand.

Chapter 45

BRON PRESSES the OFF switch on the computer while Vern powers down the generator. When the thrum of the machine stops, all Bron can hear is the high-pitched hum of happy kids, along with rousing laughter and excited conversation from the grown-ups in three languages — English, Spanish, and Spanglish. And then, in the distance...

... the fly-like buzz of a different engine.

Below in the flats, a single headlight weaves through scrub brush and cactus, then disappears from sight, the engine sound muffled, as it climbs the road to the plateau.

Suddenly, a motorbike bounds into view at the edge of the crowd, fishtailing to a stop about ten feet from Bron.

The helmet is black. The rider pulls it off and hangs it on the handlebar.

Her hair is straighter now — like in the black-and-white photos. But the freckles are back.

Bron feels like the breath has been sucked right out of him. The night is cool, but he's suddenly sweating.

His mouth is dry and there's a burn in the back of his throat.

Sunny walks toward him, then stops. The whole crowd is watching, but it's like they're not even there.

"I came to congratulate Gonzalo. I didn't think you'd be here."

"That makes two of us," says Bron.

They stare at each other for a few very long seconds.

"I'm sorry," says Sunny. "I'm sorry for everything. I was part of something that wasn't real—and when it turned real for me, I ran."

She takes a few steps closer. She's now within arm's reach.

"If you want me to leave for good, I will. I'll get back on that bike and ride right out of here. It's up to you."

Bron is really bad at this stuff. He reaches for her, but only manages to place his hands stiffly on her shoulders, like some kind of dancing robot.

Sunny gives out one soft burst of that beautiful laugh. She pulls his hands down around her waist, where they belong. She steps right up close, wraps her arms around his neck, and kisses him. Soft. Deep. Real.

A few of the eighth-grade boys whistle. The whole town applauds.

Luke and Timo clap the loudest. Even though the Mazda is good to go, they're not going anywhere. The town has kind of grown on them. Especially the bar. Which they just bought. Turns out, this acting stuff can pay pretty well.

Chapter 46

Six months later

It's not *CNN Breaking News*. It's just filler—a little human-interest story with a science twist. Correspondent Lisa Ling drew the short straw. It took her a day and a half just to get to the location. Now she's standing in the middle of a dusty desert street, trying not to sweat through her pancake makeup. She holds the mic firmly under her chin and does a walk-and-talk toward the camera:

It's a town so small, it doesn't even have a name. Population, seven hundred.

And until this week, it was pretty much stuck in the Stone Age. It's so remote, there was no cell reception, no cable service, and only a few primitive landlines. And, if you can believe it—just a single computer. But today, that's all changed…thanks to a special dedicated communications satellite, designed, built, and donated by Bron Aerospace.

The report cuts to a pan of the Bron Aerospace logo, then dissolves to stock footage of an Atlas rocket launch, then back to Ling in a tight close-up.

That means big changes for businesses and for families here in the middle of nowhere...and especially for the schoolchildren...

The shot widens to show Ling surrounded by a crowd of kids, all holding up laptops and iPads.

...maybe our next generation of aerospace engineers. I'm Lisa Ling, for CNN.

Her eyes hold the camera, waiting for the clear sign. Behind her, a very happy ten-year-old boy jumps up into frame for an epic photo bomb—holding up an ornery rooster.

Chapter 47

BRON NEVER thought about buying a house. He was just fine with the two-bedroom luxury condo. And he certainly never thought about buying a place out here in the middle of the desert. But it turns out he really likes the quiet. And the open sky.

He and Sunny are resting on matching recliners in front of the glowing embers of their fire pit. They've turned off every light in the house and around the helicopter pad so they can get the best possible view of the heavens.

"Where is it?" she says. "Show me."

Bron leans over toward her and extends his arm. You see Andromeda there, right above Polaris?

"I do." She is now an absolute master of the sky chart—so good she could almost teach Bron's astronomy lecture on her own.

Bron checks his watch. "At this time of night, this time of year, it's probably passing by right between those two points about...now."

Of course, he's exactly right. Twenty-two thousand

miles up, a gleaming communications satellite rotates slowly to reorient its solar panels. The bright light of tomorrow's morning exposes the name stenciled in huge block letters on the side panel:

SUNNY-2

Chapter 48

Near Wilmington, Mass.

"...SUNNY-2"

I type the final words and pull the page from my Selectric. I place the page on top of the manuscript pile.

Pretty good ending, if I do say so myself. Even if it wasn't entirely my idea. I think I write better back here in the civilized world—if you can call my house civilized. At least I can get a meatball grinder and the Celtics scores whenever I want.

And in my world, finishing a book calls for a beer.

Before I can even complete the thought, a frosty Corona appears in front of me.

"See? I told you he'd figure his life out for himself," says Daisy. "All you had to do was write it down."

Of course, she's right. She's been right on just about everything all along. It just took me a while to realize it.

She bought my books when nobody else did. Big points there. She got Tyler Bron to trust me with his life. Not easy. She built me up when I thought I was going nowhere.

And, no shock—she's one hell of a wedding planner.

Daisy leans over me, her dark hair spilling across my neck. We kiss. She stands back up and pulls her hair away from her face. She walks toward the bedroom.

"Coming, Shakespeare?"

I watch. Then I follow.

Daisy Crane. My beautiful, brilliant wife.

If you ask me, there's no better sight in the whole universe.

About the Authors

JAMES PATTERSON is one of the best-known and biggest-selling writers of all time. His books have sold in excess of 325 million copies worldwide. He is the author of some of the most popular series of the past two decades – the Alex Cross, Women's Murder Club, Detective Michael Bennett and Private novels – and he has written many other number one bestsellers including romance novels and stand-alone thrillers.

James is passionate about encouraging children to read. Inspired by his own son who was a reluctant reader, he also writes a range of books for young readers including the Middle School, I Funny, Treasure Hunters, House of Robots, Confessions and Maximum Ride series. James has donated millions in grants to independent bookshops and he has been the most borrowed author in UK libraries for the past ten years in a row. He lives in Florida with his wife and son.

FRANK CONSTANTINI is a writer/director, artist, and musician living in Jacksonville Beach, Florida, and Copper Mountain, Colorado, with his dog, Ozzie.

EMILY RAYMOND is the coauthor, with James Patterson, of *First Love* and *Witch & Wizard: The Lost*, as well as the ghostwriter of numerous novels for young adults. She lives in Portland, Oregon, with her family.

BRIAN SITTS is a freelance writer and former advertising creative director. He lives in Peekskill, New York, with his family.

A deadly conspiracy is working against
Detective Lindsay Boxer and soon she could
be the one on trial . . .

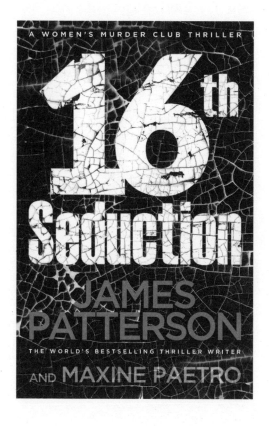

Read on for an extract.

THE MAN KNOWN AS J.

*T*HAT MUGGY morning in July my partner, Rich Conklin, and I were on stakeout in the Tenderloin, one of San Francisco's sketchiest, most crime-ridden neighborhoods. We had parked our 1998 gray Chevy sedan where we had a good view of the six-story apartment building on the corner of Leavenworth and Turk.

It's been said that watching paint dry is high entertainment compared with being on stakeout, but this was the exception to the rule.

We were psyched and determined.

We had just been assigned to a counterterrorism task force reporting back to Warren Jacobi, chief of police, and also Dean Reardon, deputy director of Homeland Security, based in DC.

This task force had been formed to address a local threat by a global terrorist group known as GAR, which had claimed credit for six sequential acts of mass terrorism in the last five days.

They were equal-ethnicity bombers, hitting three holy places—a mosque, a cathedral, and a synagogue—as well as two universities and an airport, killing over nine hundred people of all ages and nationalities in six countries.

As we understood it, GAR (Great Antiestablishment Reset) had sprung from the rubble of Middle Eastern terror groups. Several surviving leaders had swept up young dissidents around the globe, including significant numbers of zealots from Western populations who'd come of age after the digital revolution.

The identities of these killers were undetectable within their home populations, since GAR's far-flung membership hid their activities inside the dark web, an internet underground perfect for gathering without meeting.

Still, they killed real people in real life.

And then they bragged.

After a year of burning, torturing, and blowing up innocent victims, GAR published their mission statement. They planned to infiltrate every country and bring down organized religion and governments and authorities of all types. Without a known supreme commander or national hub to target, blocking this open-source terrorism had been as effective as grasping poison gas in your hand.

Because of GAR's unrelenting murderous activities, San Francisco, like most large cities, was on high alert on that Fourth of July weekend.

Conklin and I had been told very little about our

assignment, only that one of the presumed GAR opera-tives, known to us as J., had recently vaulted to the number one spot on our government's watch list.

Over the last few days J. had been spotted going in and out of the dun-colored tenement on the corner of Turk and Leavenworth, the one with laddered fire escapes on two sides and a lone tree growing out of the pavement beside the front door.

Our instructions were to watch for him. If we saw him, we were to report his activities by radio, even as eyes in the skies were on this intersection from an AFB in Nevada or Arizona or Washington, DC.

It was a watch-only assignment, and when a male fig-ure matching the grainy image we had — of a bearded man, five foot nine, hat shading his face — left the dun-colored apartment building, we took note.

When this character crossed to our side of the street and got into a white refrigerator van parked in front of the T.L. Market and Deli, we phoned it in.

Conklin and I have been partners for so many years and can almost read each other's minds. We exchanged a look and knew that we couldn't just *watch* a suspected terrorist pull out into our streets without doing something about it.

I said, "Following is watching."

Rich said, "Just a second, Lindsay. Okay?"

His conversation with the deputy was short. Rich gave me the thumbs-up and I started up the car. We pulled out two cars lengths behind the white van driven by a presumed high-level terrorist known as J.

I EDGED our sharklike Chevy along Turk and turned left on Hyde, keeping just far enough behind J.'s van to stay out of his rearview while keeping an eye on him. After following him through a couple of turns, I lost the van at a stop light on Tenth Street. I had to make a split-second decision whether or not to run the light.

My decision was *Go*.

My hands were sweating on the wheel as I shot through the intersection and was blasted by a cacophony of horns, which called attention to us. I didn't enjoy that at all.

Conklin said, "There he is."

The white van was hemmed in by other vehicles traveling at something close to the speed limit. I kept it in our sights from a good distance behind the pack. And then the van merged into US Route 101 South toward San Jose.

The highway was a good, wide road with enough traffic to ensure that J. would never pick our Chevy out of the flow.

Conklin worked the radio communications, deftly switching channels between chief of police Warren

Jacobi and DHS deputy director Dean Reardon, who was three time zones away. Dispatch kept us updated on the movements of other units in our task force that were now part of a staggered caravan weaving between lanes, taking turns at stepping on the gas, then falling back.

We followed J.'s van under the sunny glare on 101 South, and after twelve miles, instead of heading down to San Jose and the Central Coast, he took the lane that funneled traffic to SFO.

Conklin had Jacobi on the line.

"Chief, he's heading toward SFO."

Several voices crackled over the radio, but I kept visual contact with the man in the van that was moving steadily toward San Francisco International Airport.

That van was now the most frightening vehicle imaginable. GAR had sensitized all of us to worst-case scenarios, and a lot of explosives could be packed into a vehicle of that size. A terrorist wouldn't have to get on a plane or even walk into an airline terminal. I could easily imagine J. crashing his vehicle through luggage check-in and ramming the plate-glass windows before setting off a bomb.

Conklin had signed off with Jacobi and now said to me, "Lindsay, SFO security has sent fire trucks and construction vehicles out to obstruct traffic on airport access roads in all directions."

Good.

I stepped on the gas and flipped on the sirens. Behind us, others in our team did the same, and I saw flashing lights getting onto the service road from the north.

Passenger cars pulled onto the shoulder to let us fly by, and within seconds we were passing J.'s van as we entered the International Departures lane.

Signs listing names of airlines appeared overhead. SFO's parking garage rose up on our right. Off-ramps and service roads circled and crossed underneath our roadway, which was now an overpass. The outline of the international terminal grew closer and larger just up ahead.

Rich and I were leading a group of cars heading to the airport when I saw cruisers heading away from the terminal right toward us.

It was a high-speed pincer movement.

J. saw what was happening and had only two choices: keep going or stop. He wrenched his wheel hard to the right and the van skidded across to the far right lane, where there was one last exit to the garage, which a hundred yards farther on had its own exit to South Link Road. The exit was open and unguarded.

I screamed to Conklin, *"Hang on!"*

I passed the white van on my right, gave the Chevy more gas, and turned the wheel hard, blocking the exit. At the last possible moment, as I was bracing for a crash, J. jerked his wheel hard left and pulled around us.

By then the airport roadway was filled with law enforcement cruisers, their lights flashing, sirens blowing.

The van screeched to a halt.

Adrenaline had sent my heart rate into the red zone, and sweat sheeted down my body.

Both my partner and I asked if the other was okay as cop cars lined up behind us and ahead of us, forming an impenetrable vehicular wall.

A security cop with a megaphone addressed J.

"Get out of the vehicle. Hands up. Get out now, buddy. No one wants to hurt you."

Would J. go ballistic?

I pictured the van going up in a fiery explosion forty feet from where I sat in an old sedan. I flashed on the image of my little girl when I saw her this morning, wearing baby-duck yellow, beating her spoon on the table. Would I ever see her again?

Just then the white van's passenger door opened and J. jumped out. A voice amplified through a bullhorn boomed, *"Don't move. Hands in the air."*

J. ignored the warning.

He ran across the four lanes and reached the concrete guardrail. He looked out over the edge. He paused.

There was nothing between him and the road below but forty feet of air.

Shots were fired.

I saw J. jump.

Rich shouted at me, *"Get down!"*

We both ducked below the dash and linked our fingers over the backs of our necks as an explosion boomed, rocking our car, setting off the car alarm, blinding us with white light.

That sick bastard had detonated his bomb.

ICH AND I sat parked in the no-parking zone outside the terminal, still reeling from what had happened an eighth of a mile from the airport terminals.

We had seen J. jump from the departures lane to a service road and knew that he had detonated his vest before he hit the pavement.

We had tried to guess what he had been thinking. Our current theory was that he hadn't wanted to be captured. He didn't want to talk.

Conklin said, "Maybe he figured jumping off the ramp, he'd land safely on a passing vehicle, like he was in a Jackie Chan movie."

I jumped when someone leaned through the car window. It was Tom Generosa, counterterrorism chief, keeping us in the loop.

He said, "Here's what we know so far. The guy you call J. had a plan to kill a lot of people inside a crowd, that's not in doubt. His vest was of the antipersonnel variety. Packed with nails and ball bearings and rat poison. That's an anticoagulant. The explosion was meant to propel the shrapnel, and it did. But the van contained the blast. The only casualty was the jumper."

I nodded and Generosa continued.

"The nails and shit shredded his body and any information he may have been carrying on his person. He left a crater and a roadway full of human tissue and shrapnel."

"And the van?" I said.

"Bomb squad cleared it. The FBI is loading it onto a flatbed, taking it to the crime lab. For starters, J. stole the van from the market on Turk. Maybe his prints will be on the steering wheel, but I won't be surprised if he can't be positively ID'd."

Generosa told us that federal agents as well as SFPD's Crime Scene Investigation Unit were at the site of the explosion now, that the CSI was processing it, and that after it was measured and photographed, the remains of the man known as J. would be transported by refrigerated van, along with explosive samples, to the FBI's and the SFPD's forensics labs.

Of course we knew that J.'s bomb had shut down SFO.

All airline passengers had been bused to other locations. Outbound flights had been grounded, and incoming flights had been rerouted to other airfields. We could see for ourselves that the terminal buildings were crawling with a multitude of law enforcement agents from CIA, FBI, DHS, and airport security, as well as their bomb-sniffing dogs.

Generosa couldn't estimate with any certainty how long SFO would be out of commission, but as bad as that was for the airlines, their passengers, and traffic, GAR hadn't scored a hit in San Francisco today.

We thanked Generosa for the report.

He told us, "Take good care," and walked over to the next car in the line behind us. We were about to call in for further instructions when our radio sputtered and Jacobi's voice filled our car. Both Conklin and I had partnered with Jacobi before his promotion to chief. It was so good to hear his voice.

He said, "You two are something else, you know? You cut J. off from his target. Thank God for that."

I said, "Man, oh, man. I can't stand to imagine it."

But I *did* imagine it. I pictured an airport in Paris. I pictured another in Turkey. I could easily see what might have gone down at SFO if J. had gotten into or even near a terminal. When I first started in Homicide, an airport bombing had been inconceivable. Now? These horrifying bombings were almost becoming commonplace.

Jacobi's voice was still coming over the radio.

He said, "Effective as soon as you turn in your report, you two are off duty. Boxer. Conklin. I'm proud of you. I love you both.

"Thanks from me and from Deputy Reardon and a lot of people who've never heard of you and never will. Many lives were saved. Stand down. Come home. The Feds are going to take it from here."

I was shaking with relief when I turned the car keys over to Conklin. I got into the passenger seat. I leaned back and closed my eyes as he drove us back to the Hall.

ONE MONTH LATER

*I*T WAS our wedding anniversary, also our first date night since Joe and I separated six months ago. Joe had surprised me, calling me up as I was leaving work, saying, "I reserved a window table. Say yes, Lindsay. I'm parked right outside."

I'd given in and now we were at the Crested Cormorant, the hot new seafood restaurant on Pier 9, with a front-row seat on San Francisco Bay. Candles flickered on tables around us as a pink sunset colored the sky to the horizon, tinting the rippling water as the mist rolled in.

Joe was talking about his youngest brother.

"So, at age forty, Petey finally meets the love of his life at a fire department car wash." He laughed. "Amanda was power-washing his whitewalls, and, somehow, that jump-starts his heart."

"You think her T-shirt got wet?"

Joe laughed again. I loved his laugh.

He said, "Very possibly. We're invited to their wedding in Cozumel next month. Think about it, okay?"

Looking into my husband's eyes, I saw how much he wanted to bring us back to our wedding in a gazebo overlooking Half Moon Bay. We'd vowed in front of dear friends and family to love each other from that day forward.

It had been a promise I knew I could keep.

But I hadn't been able to see around corners, not then. Now, in this romantic setting, Joe was hoping for magic to strike again. As for me, my innocence was gone.

I wished it weren't so.

I was conflicted. Should I reach across the table, squeeze Joe's hand, and tell him to come home? Or was it time for us both to admit that our Humpty Dumpty marriage couldn't be put back together again?

Joe lifted his wineglass and said, "To happy days."

Just then there was a sharp sound—as if the world had cracked open—followed by the boom of rolling thunder and a bright flash on the neighboring pier.

I screamed, "Nooooo!"

I grabbed Joe's arm and stared openmouthed across the water to Pier 15, the site of Scientific-Tron, a science museum, called Sci-Tron for short. It was a massive, geometric glass-and-steel structure designed for human interaction with the past and especially the future. The structure was unfolding like a bud bursting into bloom right in front of my eyes. Metal panels flew toward us, a mushroom cloud formed over Pier 15, and an overarching hail of glinting glass shards fell into the bay.

Joe said, *"Jesus. What the hell?"* his expression perfectly mirroring the horror I felt. *Another bomb.*

Sci-Tron was open to the public seven days a week but to adults only on Thursday nights. This was Thursday, wasn't it? Yes. People were inside the museum.

Was this a GAR attack? Had to be.

Joe threw down a credit card, then stabbed at his phone and called his job. Similarly, I called SFPD dispatch and reported what looked to be a mass casualty incident.

"There's been an explosion with fire at Sci-Tron, Pier 15. Send all cars. FD. Bomb squad. Ambulances. And find Lieutenant Brady. Tell him I'm on the scene."

Joe said, "Lindsay, wait here. I'll be back—"

"You're kidding."

"You want to get killed?"

"Do *you?*"

I followed Joe out of the restaurant onto the walkway that ran the length of the pier. We stood for a long moment at the railing and watched Sci-Tron's two-story metal-frame structure crumple as the roof caved in.

The sight was devastating and almost impossible to believe, but it was real. Sci-Tron had been blown up.

Joe and I started running.

JAMES PATTERSON
BOOK**SHOTS**

stories at the speed of life

BOOK**SHOTS** are page-turning stories by James Patterson and other writers that can be read in one sitting.

Each and every one is fast-paced, 100% story-driven; a shot of pure entertainment guaranteed to satisfy.

Under 150 pages
Under £3

Available as new, compact paperbacks, ebooks and audio, everywhere books are sold.

For more details, visit: **www.bookshots.com**

BOOK**SHOTS**
THE ULTIMATE FORM OF STORYTELLING.
FROM THE ULTIMATE STORYTELLER.

Also by James Patterson

ALEX CROSS NOVELS

Along Came a Spider • Kiss the Girls • Jack and Jill •
Cat and Mouse • Pop Goes the Weasel • Roses are Red •
Violets are Blue • Four Blind Mice • The Big Bad Wolf •
London Bridges • Mary, Mary • Cross • Double Cross •
Cross Country • Alex Cross's Trial (*with Richard DiLallo*) •
I, Alex Cross • Cross Fire • Kill Alex Cross • Merry
Christmas, Alex Cross • Alex Cross, Run • Cross My
Heart • Hope to Die • Cross Justice • Cross the Line

THE WOMEN'S MURDER CLUB SERIES

1st to Die • 2nd Chance (*with Andrew Gross*) • 3rd Degree
(*with Andrew Gross*) • 4th of July (*with Maxine Paetro*) •
The 5th Horseman (*with Maxine Paetro*) • The 6th Target
(*with Maxine Paetro*) • 7th Heaven (*with Maxine Paetro*) •
8th Confession (*with Maxine Paetro*) • 9th Judgement (*with
Maxine Paetro*) • 10th Anniversary (*with Maxine Paetro*) •
11th Hour (*with Maxine Paetro*) • 12th of Never (*with Maxine
Paetro*) • Unlucky 13 (*with Maxine Paetro*) • 14th Deadly Sin
(*with Maxine Paetro*) • 15th Affair (*with Maxine Paetro*) •
16th Seduction (*with Maxine Paetro*)

DETECTIVE MICHAEL BENNETT SERIES

Step on a Crack (*with Michael Ledwidge*) • Run for Your Life
(*with Michael Ledwidge*) • Worst Case (*with Michael Ledwidge*) •
Tick Tock (*with Michael Ledwidge*) • I, Michael Bennett
(*with Michael Ledwidge*) • Gone (*with Michael Ledwidge*) •
Burn (*with Michael Ledwidge*) • Alert (*with Michael Ledwidge*) •
Bullseye (*with Michael Ledwidge*)

PRIVATE NOVELS

Private (*with Maxine Paetro*) • Private London (*with Mark
Pearson*) • Private Games (*with Mark Sullivan*) • Private: No. 1

Suspect (*with Maxine Paetro*) • Private Berlin (*with Mark Sullivan*) • Private Down Under (*with Michael White*) • Private L.A. (*with Mark Sullivan*) • Private India (*with Ashwin Sanghi*) • Private Vegas (*with Maxine Paetro*) • Private Sydney (*with Kathryn Fox*) • Private Paris (*with Mark Sullivan*) • The Games (*with Mark Sullivan*) • Private Delhi (*with Ashwin Sanghi*)

NYPD RED SERIES

NYPD Red (*with Marshall Karp*) • NYPD Red 2 (*with Marshall Karp*) • NYPD Red 3 (*with Marshall Karp*) • NYPD Red 4 (*with Marshall Karp*)

DETECTIVE HARRIET BLUE SERIES

Never Never (*with Candice Fox*) • Fifty Fifty (*with Candice Fox, to be published July 2017*)

NON-FICTION

Torn Apart (*with Hal and Cory Friedman*) • The Murder of King Tut (*with Martin Dugard*)

STAND-ALONE THRILLERS

The Thomas Berryman Number Sail (*with Howard Roughan*) • Swimsuit (*with Maxine Paetro*) • Don't Blink (*with Howard Roughan*) • Postcard Killers (*with Liza Marklund*) • Toys (*with Neil McMahon*) • Now You See Her (*with Michael Ledwidge*) • Kill Me If You Can (*with Marshall Karp*) • Guilty Wives (*with David Ellis*) • Zoo (*with Michael Ledwidge*) • Second Honeymoon (*with Howard Roughan*) • Mistress (*with David Ellis*) • Invisible (*with David Ellis*) • Truth or Die (*with Howard Roughan*) • Murder House (*with David Ellis*) • Woman of God (*with Maxine Paetro*) • Hide and Seek • Humans, Bow Down (*with Emily Raymond*)

OTHER TITLES

Miracle at Augusta (*with Peter de Jonge*)

FAMILY OF PAGE-TURNERS

MIDDLE SCHOOL BOOKS

The Worst Years of My Life (*with Chris Tebbetts*) • Get Me Out of Here! (*with Chris Tebbetts*) • My Brother Is a Big, Fat Liar (*with Lisa Papademetriou*) • How I Survived Bullies, Broccoli, and Snake Hill (*with Chris Tebbetts*) • Ultimate Showdown (*with Julia Bergen*) • Save Rafe! (*with Chris Tebbetts*) • Just My Rotten Luck (*with Chris Tebbetts*) • Dog's Best Friend (*with Chris Tebbetts*) • Escape to Australia (*with Martin Chatterton*)

I FUNNY SERIES

I Funny (*with Chris Grabenstein*) • I Even Funnier (*with Chris Grabenstein*) • I Totally Funniest (*with Chris Grabenstein*) • I Funny TV (*with Chris Grabenstein*) • School of Laughs (*with Chris Grabenstein*)

TREASURE HUNTERS SERIES

Treasure Hunters (*with Chris Grabenstein*) • Danger Down the Nile (*with Chris Grabenstein*) • Secret of the Forbidden City (*with Chris Grabenstein*) • Peril at the Top of the World (*with Chris Grabenstein*)

HOUSE OF ROBOTS SERIES

House of Robots (*with Chris Grabenstein*) • Robots Go Wild! (*with Chris Grabenstein*) • Robot Revolution (*with Chris Grabenstein*)

OTHER ILLUSTRATED NOVELS

Kenny Wright: Superhero (*with Chris Tebbetts*) • Homeroom Diaries (*with Lisa Papademetriou*) • Jacky Ha-Ha (*with Chris Grabenstein*) • Word of Mouse (*with Chris Grabenstein*)

MAXIMUM RIDE SERIES

The Angel Experiment • School's Out Forever • Saving the World and Other Extreme Sports • The Final Warning • Max • Fang • Angel • Nevermore • Forever

CONFESSIONS SERIES

Confessions of a Murder Suspect (*with Maxine Paetro*) • The Private School Murders (*with Maxine Paetro*) • The Paris Mysteries (*with Maxine Paetro*) • The Murder of an Angel (*with Maxine Paetro*)

WITCH & WIZARD SERIES

Witch & Wizard (*with Gabrielle Charbonnet*) • The Gift (*with Ned Rust*) • The Fire (*with Jill Dembowski*) • The Kiss (*with Jill Dembowski*) • The Lost (*with Emily Raymond*)

DANIEL X SERIES

The Dangerous Days of Daniel X (*with Michael Ledwidge*) • Watch the Skies (*with Ned Rust*) • Demons and Druids (*with Adam Sadler*) • Game Over (*with Ned Rust*) • Armageddon (*with Chris Grabenstein*) • Lights Out (*with Chris Grabenstein*)

GRAPHIC NOVELS

Daniel X: Alien Hunter (*with Leopoldo Gout*) • Maximum Ride: Manga Vols. 1–9 (*with NaRae Lee*)

For more information about James Patterson's novels, visit www.jamespatterson.co.uk

Or become a fan on Facebook